PRAISE FOR

THE DOCTOR OF BELLECHESTER

The year is 1959. The place is London. Mary Elizabeth Senty, sometimes known as Miss Emme and Dr. Senty, is a young woman from a farm in central Minnesota who is in her fourth year of residency in a teaching hospital in London. By chance, she meets Harold Merton, an elderly man who seems to be suffering from the intense August heat. . . . Miss Emme and Harold quickly strike up a friendship, drawn together in part by their strong Catholic faith. But in spite of that friendship, they don't reveal much about themselves. . . . The story raises one question after another, and only gradually reveals the answers both to the main characters and to the readers. *The Doctor of Bellechester* also reveals a world in which women in medicine were rare. . . encouraging readers to reflect on the characters and the choices they make and to look for intersections between the events in the story and their lives.

—*Mara Faulkner, OSB*
Professor Emerita, College of St. Benedict

The Doctor of Bellechester [has] great character development, pacing, and a gentle approach to the societal issues of aging challenges and gender discrimination. . . . It will be very appealing to women readers who grew up experiencing gender discrimination in education and in the workplace. . . . and readers who enjoy quality storytelling about people of faith. I loved Harold Merton and Emme Senty. . . . Harold was believable because of his vulnerabilities. I could really identify with Emme for trying so hard to be the "perfect" physician. You and I know a lot of women who tried their very best in a world dominated by powerful men!

—*Sharon L. Tomlin, EdD, Catholic Educator & Avid Reader*

Bob and I both enjoyed your novel. . . We found the font and text layout . . . beautiful and easy to read. The pacing of your clear language and character development drew us through the story. It was a perfect book to relax with on a weekend as we could easily see the people and setting and get caught up in the world you created.

—*L.E. Dahlhoff, EdD, Catholic educator, and R.F. Swenson Esq, researcher, both avid readers of historical fiction*

The *Doctor of Bellechester* by Margaret A. Blenkush is a pleasant read with likeable main characters. It is just the book to curl up with on cold winter evenings or to take with you on a vacation. The setting is an English hospital, where Dr. Merton is in search of a junior doctor to replace him when he retires from his practice in the small town of Bellechester. A touch of mystery now and then—especially concerning a kind young woman—creates suspense and engages readers. Just the right amount of description facilitates visualizing the story as it unfolds. Realistically, issues related to women today surface here in 1959 as well. Fans of medical stories and shows in particular will be pleased with the book's details of hospital life and treatments. Although the book can stand alone, readers can anticipate following the adventures of Dr. M.E. Senty in the rest of the series.

—*Mary Kathleen Glavich, SND, author, editor, speaker*

THE DOCTOR OF BELLECHESTER

Book 1

BY MARGARET A. BLENKUSH

To Debi,

May all your dreams come true.

Margaret A. Blenkush

Enjoy

Edited by Courtney King Bain
Cover Illustration by Lisa Kosmo

ISBN 13: 978-1-64343-690-6
Library of Congress Catalog Number: 2022902915
Printed in the United States of America

First Printing: 2022
26   25   24   23   22   5   4   3   2   1

Book design and typesetting by Tina Brackins
This book is typeset in Adobe Jenson Pro and Poetica.

Pond Reads Press
939 Seventh Street West
Saint Paul, MN 55102
(952) 829-8818
www.BeaversPondPress.com

Contact Margaret A. Blenkush at margaretablenkush.com for school visits, speaking engagements, book club discussions, and interviews.

BOOK DEDICATION

Sister Emily Devine, rsm (1938–2021)

Em was a faithful Sister of Mercy for over sixty-two years

>   a fearless advocate for peace and justice
>   a fantastic basketball player
>   and a loyal friend for over forty years

Without her encouragement and unflagging confidence in me, this book would never have been written.

Contents

$\mathcal{F}$OREWORD

Welcome, readers, to my first novel. I hope you enjoy reading it as much as I enjoyed writing it. The story takes place in 1959, and I tried to be as true to the times as possible. For example, in 1959, English trains and commercial buildings were not air-conditioned. Even today, most English hospitals do not have air-conditioning.

I took literary license with the set-up of the hospital. In the 1950s, English hospitals had wards where there were many beds in a large room. Semi-private or private rooms were not the norm. Nurses would have their stations at the head of the ward. For the purpose of advancing the plot of this story, Mother of Mercy Hospital is designed with private rooms and a centralized nursing station.

The English system for training general practitioners (GPs) of the 1950s consisted of a four-year program after doctors graduated from medical school. They were known as junior doctors. They were fully qualified but must still practice under supervision. This would be similar to the U.S. program of interns and residents. After junior doctors successfully completed this program, they took an exam to become members of The Royal College of General Practitioners. Members were then designated as GPs and could practice independently.

A simple act of kindness can change a life. In this story, maybe two lives? Get comfortable, sit back, and enjoy *The Doctor of Bellechester*.

Monday, August 24, 1959, London

CHAPTER 1

HAROLD'S LONDON ADVENTURE

In 1959, London sweltered under the hot August sun. A taxicab pulled up to the front of London's Mother of Mercy Hospital, and a man in his early sixties emerged from the cab carrying a small brown suitcase. He was of average height and stocky build, and his shoulders stooped as if a heavy burden had lain on his back for a very long time. His rumpled tan suit was damp with sweat. After he paid the driver, Dr. Harold Merton stood on the sidewalk and looked up at the imposing seven-story structure in front of him. The U-shaped building took up an entire city block. In the middle stood a fountain and a few benches. Flower beds bursting with the blooms of summer annuals provided the only color to the area. Farther back, at the entrance of the building, were multiple revolving doors that were always turning as people went in and out. The constant circular movement of the doors was hypnotic. People walked hurriedly and confidently. They knew where they were going. Harold set his suitcase down, took out his handkerchief, and wiped the dripping sweat off his face and his balding head. Doubts filled his mind and overtook his entire body. He knew he should move, but the soles of his shoes seemed to have melted into the sidewalk and the hypnotic doors had put him in a daze. He was still standing there staring at the building when he heard an angelic voice say, "Hello. Can I help you?"

Turning toward the voice, he saw not a celestial being but a young woman whom he guessed was about thirty years of age. She wore a frilly white blouse with capped short sleeves and a navy pencil skirt. Her brown hair was pulled back in a bun at the nape of her neck. As she stood before him,

Harold saw the expression on her face change from a carefree smile to a look of concern. Her blue eyes narrowed, her brow furrowed, and her lips pursed together as she studied him carefully. Harold, wide-eyed, just stared at her.

"Here, let's get you out of the sun." She picked up his suitcase and gently took his arm, guiding him across the street to the city park. Searching for a moment, she found a bench in the shade. "Now you just sit here for a few minutes and rest. I'll be back as quickly as I can. Now, promise me that you won't move until I return." She set his suitcase down next to him. Harold could only nod. She seemed satisfied and quickly crossed the street in the middle of the block, disappearing into one of a row of shops.

Harold took out his handkerchief and wiped his face again. In his mind, he tried to reconstruct the events of the morning. He had begun his journey in high spirits, feeling a sense of excitement he had not felt in a very long time. After a pleasant fifteen-minute drive, he parked his car at the Craven Arms depot and waited for the train that would take him into London. The day was clear and sunny. Even at that hour, Harold could tell it was going to be an unseasonably warm day. Luckily, he found a bench in the shade to wait for the train, which arrived at 8:15 a.m. and was only half full. He was thankful he found an empty row of seats, so he did not have to engage in conversation with anyone. After storing his suitcase into the bin above his seat, he sank down by the window, which had been pulled partially down, and watched the scenery pass by. There was plenty of time to think. Maybe there was too much time to think. As the train traveled past the rolling hills and small farms, it took him farther from home. He began to have second thoughts.

When he'd hatched his plan a month ago, it had all seemed so simple and very logical. Rather than advertising in some medical journal for a doctor to join his practice, he had decided to call up his classmate from medical school, Dr. Basil Applegate. Basil was now head of the junior doctors at Mother of Mercy Hospital in London. Basil was most agreeable to have Harold come and interview his fourth-year junior doctors. Their time at the hospital would conclude at the end of August, and Basil was confident that Harold would find a young doctor to join him in Bellechester.

In Newport, Harold had to change trains. While waiting for the London train to arrive, he'd wandered into the gift shop and made a few purchases for the journey. The train had pulled out of the station at 10:40 a.m., beginning the final leg of his journey. As the day lengthened and the sun rose higher in the sky, the train car started to heat up. As the train got closer to London, the scenery changed from open spaces to factories to row upon row of houses. His precious solitude was interrupted as more passengers got on the train. He'd forced himself to exchange pleasantries with his seatmate. Everything had seemed to close in on him. The heat of the day had made him uncomfortable and brought more doubts and misgivings to his mind.

By the time the train had reached Paddington Station, Harold was totally discombobulated. He could not even remember the last time he had visited London. He had forgotten how different the pace of life was in the big city compared to his small rural village.

When he'd departed the train, the crush of the crowds in the station had pressed in on him and carried him along. When he'd finally been spat from the train station, it was early afternoon. Everything had seemed to assault his senses: the buildings were so tall, they blocked out the sun. Instead of breathing in the sweet country air, his nostrils were assaulted with the putrid smells of fermenting garbage and car exhaust. His ears were blasted with the sounds of the traffic and their blaring car horns, drills chewing up concrete, and the snatches of conversation as groups of people passed along the sidewalks.

The heat and humidity of the day continued to be oppressive. Not only was the air hot and sticky but the heat was radiating off the stone buildings, coming up from the pavement and streets. Surrounded by the heat, Harold felt like he was in the throes of hell. He'd secured a taxicab a block from the train station, and the taxi had deposited him at his final destination, Mother of Mercy Hospital. Harold remembered exiting the taxi and looking up at the hospital. But he was still a bit foggy on how he had landed on this bench in the park. Then he remembered that there was a young woman. He smiled to himself when he thought she was an angel. Harold looked at his watch and saw the time—2:12 p.m. It felt good to be sitting in the shade. His appointment with Dr. Applegate was set for three o'clock. Plenty of time for a little rest. As he was thinking these thoughts, the angelic young woman reappeared.

"I'm so glad you're still here," she said as she sat down beside him. "Here now, I brought you a bottle of water with lemon. That will help rehydrate you. I had Alex, my friend at my favorite neighborhood restaurant, mix us up a batch, enough for two bottles. And his mother, the chef there, makes the best cold chicken sandwiches in town."

"Thank you, but you didn't have to go through all that bother for me," Harold said as he took the items from her. Sitting in the shade revived his spirits a bit. He started to feel more like himself again.

"Oh yes, I did. You looked like you were ready to keel over from the heat, and I couldn't have you lying on the sidewalk. How would that look? Not a good image for the hospital. Bad for business, don't you think?" she said kindly and with a smile.

"Do you work at the hospital?" Harold asked. Surprisingly, he forgot his shyness. He found it easy to converse with her.

"Indeed, I've been there for over four years now." She unwrapped her sandwich, but kept the paper wrapping around the bottom, eating just a neat row across the top, making no mess as she ate. "Will you be staying with us long?" she asked as she nodded toward his suitcase.

"Just a couple of days, I think. It depends on how things go," he replied.

Harold hadn't realized how hungry and thirsty he had been. He couldn't even remember the last time he'd had an alfresco lunch. The sandwich was delicious. His mind wandered, and he wondered what his friend Matt would say when he told him he'd had lunch in the park with a beautiful young lady. Matt—or Father Mathias

Evenson, as he was usually known by the villagers—was his closest friend and confidant in Bellechester. Harold imagined Matt falling off his chair in shock at the news!

Harold snuck another look over to her, just to satisfy himself that she wasn't a heavenly apparition, when he noticed her looking at him with an expectant expression on her face. "Excuse me, did you ask me something?" Harold asked. He was a bit embarrassed, as he realized he had lost himself in his thoughts again and was not paying attention.

"I had just asked you if you have family or friends who will be visiting you while you are in the hospital. I don't mean to pry, but you seem to be on your own," she said.

This time, Harold made sure he listened carefully. Usually, he was a very private person, but she asked the question so matter-of-factly and without any judgment that he found himself answering without hesitation. "Yes, I came to London by myself. No family. Besides Dr. Basil Applegate, I don't know anyone in London."

"Oh, Dr. Applegate!" she exclaimed. "He is one of my favorite people. He is a very good doctor and a very decent human being. He will take excellent care of you. But," she said, "I was not aware he saw patients privately. He is director of junior doctors and so spends all of his time teaching and directing their work."

"Dr. Applegate is an old friend," Harold replied, and he looked at his watch. It read 2:42 p.m. "Oh my, I should be going. My appointment with Dr. Applegate is for three o'clock. I don't want to be late, and since I have no idea where I am going, I need to leave extra time to get lost." He smiled and rose to leave, picking up his waste as he gathered his things. "But thank you for the lunch and the conversation. I feel much better now, Miss . . ."

"Emme," she answered, giving him her nickname instead of her full name.

Harold repeated, "Miss Emme." He bowed and extended his hand. "And I am Harold Merton. So glad to have made your acquaintance." In London, it was easy to avoid the intimacy of full disclosure, so Harold did not feel the necessity to reveal his title.

Mary Elizabeth took his hand and said, "It has been a pleasure to meet you too, Mr. Harold Merton." She continued, "But you aren't getting rid of me that fast. No, I will escort you to Dr. Applegate's office. Turns out, I am going that way anyway, and I want to make sure you get there. Here, I will take your empty bottle. I promised Alex I would return them. Now, you just sit down again, and I will be back shortly. May I tell him how you enjoyed the sandwich?" She quickly gathered her trash, deposited it in the barrel, and returned to stand beside him.

"Of course," Harold replied. "Please give my compliments to Alex's mother. It truly was the best sandwich I have ever eaten. It helped revive this old man's spirits." Harold surprised himself by the words that came out of his mouth next: "Before I go back home, Miss Emme, I hope we can have lunch together again. Then it will be my treat. I truly enjoyed talking with you."

"Why, Mr. Merton, that would be wonderful. I shall look forward to it," Mary Elizabeth replied and flashed an ear-to-ear smile. "Now, you just sit here for a moment while I run and return these bottles." Harold did as he was told.

She was true to her word, and Harold had to wait only a few minutes before she returned. As they walked toward the hospital, he asked in a concerned tone, "I have been thinking, Miss Emme, how will I ever find you again?"

"Don't worry, Mr. Merton," Mary Elizabeth reassured him. "Remember, this is my hospital. I will find you. May I give you some advice to ensure you have a pleasant hospital stay?"

"Please. It has been so long since I have been in a hospital like this . . ." Harold's voice trailed off as he stopped and once again looked up at the massive building in front of him.

Mary Elizabeth slipped her arm under his and moved him forward. Harold had no choice but to follow her lead. She spoke confidently. "Now, Mr. Merton, listen carefully. Number one: remember that there are lots of good people working in this building. Their job is to take care of you. They are professionals. They know what they are doing. Number two: Dr. Applegate will probably assign you a junior doctor. Be sure you insist on a fourth-year junior doctor to attend you. He might try to pawn off a third-year on you, but you hold your ground. Remember, only fourth-year junior doctors. I happen to know for a fact that there are some very competent doctors in that group. Number three: don't be afraid to ask your doctor questions about your condition or any procedures that may be ordered for you. Any doctor worth his or her salt should be able to answer your questions to your satisfaction. And number four: you have to be your own best advocate. Don't be afraid to speak up, ask for what you need."

Harold smiled. "That is all very good advice. I will try to remember. Thank you." By now, they had arrived at the revolving doors. Mary Elizabeth went first, and she waited in the lobby for Harold to catch up to her. The lobby was large and bright, as there was no outer wall, just floor-to-ceiling windows. The marble floor had so much polish that Harold felt as if he were walking on ice. Mary Elizabeth walked past the first set of lifts, where a crowd of people was waiting, to a second set of lifts at the rear of the lobby. She pressed the button, and the doors opened. They were the only two occupants who got in, and Mary Elizabeth reached across Harold to press the button for the seventh floor.

As the lift was ascending, Harold said, "I appreciate you taking me to my appointment."

"Well, I was going up to the seventh floor anyway, so it was no trouble."

"What do you do here at the hospital? Are you a secretary?"

"No," she replied. She smiled vaguely, saying nothing more. The lift stopped, and she said, "Oh, here we are!" The doors opened, and immediately the smell of bedpans and antiseptic greeted them. Mary Elizabeth led Harold down the hall to the end and turned to the left. She stopped at the first door. She turned to Harold and said, "This is where I leave you. Mrs. Stanfield is inside. She is Dr. Applegate's secretary. She will take care of you." Mary Elizabeth then took Harold's hand and looked him in the eyes. "Now, don't worry, Mr. Merton. You are in good hands. Good luck to you." She dropped his hand, smiled, and went on her way down the hall.

CHAPTER 2

OLD FRIENDS MEET AGAIN

Harold stood at the door of Dr. Applegate's office for a moment and watched Mary Elizabeth until she disappeared behind a set of swinging doors before he turned the knob and walked in. Harold walked up to the attractive middle-aged woman, who was busily typing a letter. "Dr. Harold Merton to see Dr. Basil Applegate," he said.

Mrs. Stanfield stopped typing and looked up at him and smiled. "Yes, Dr. Merton. Dr. Applegate is expecting you." She got up and escorted Harold to an inner door and knocked.

"Come in," called a rich baritone voice.

Mrs. Stanfield opened the door and walked into the room. Harold, still carrying his suitcase, followed her. When Dr. Applegate saw Harold, he jumped out of his chair to greet him.

Dr. Applegate was a large, energetic man. He stood at least six foot four. He had a head of thick silver hair and a face whose wrinkles indicated he smiled often. His blue eyes seemed to dance. "Harold, so nice to see you again. It has been too long." He shook Harold's hand heartily. "Come, have a seat. Would you like something to drink? Tea? Something cold, perhaps? My goodness, it is good to see you again."

Harold smiled. "Very good to see you again too, Basil. A glass of water would hit the spot. Thank you." He sat in the chair offered to him.

Dr. Applegate went back around and sat behind his massive desk. "Mrs. Stanfield, if you please, could you bring us two glasses of water?"

"Of course, Doctor. Would you like me to bring you anything else?"

Dr. Applegate looked inquiringly over to Harold. Harold replied, "No, thank you. I had a late lunch."

"No, Mrs. Stanfield, just the waters. Thank you."

Mrs. Stanfield left the two men alone. When the door closed, Dr. Applegate said, "I must say, Harold, I was quite surprised when I got your phone call last month. What's all this about wanting to interview my fourth-year junior doctors?"

Harold said, "Bellechester is no longer the sleepy little village it was when I arrived thirty years ago. It is growing. I am not sure I can keep up anymore. This past year was very difficult, as we suffered through a particularly severe flu season. Recently, I have been feeling my age, and I would like to retire in a few years. I just want to be sure I will be leaving Bellechester in capable hands. So, I am here to see whether I can find a qualified doctor I can mentor and who will, one day, take my place."

Just then, there was a knock on the door. Dr. Applegate called, "Come in." Mrs. Stanfield came in with the water and handed one to Harold and the other to Dr. Applegate. "Thank you, Mrs. Stanfield. Please hold my calls."

"Yes, Doctor," Mrs. Stanfield replied and left them alone again.

When the door was closed, Dr. Applegate said, "While I have an exceptional group of fourth-year junior doctors, I am afraid almost all of them have already received offers for next year. One is going back to his native India to set up practice. Another has been offered a post-residency fellowship at a major medical institution in the United States. A third will be joining his family's practice here in London. The fourth is waiting to hear about a research position, and the fifth is still looking, although I hear he has several interviews lined up. Would you like to interview him?"

As Dr. Applegate talked, Harold's face fell. "Yes, I suppose so. You sounded so optimistic on the phone that I would find someone."

"Harold," Dr. Applegate said gently, "we spoke last month. All of these appointments have happened in the last few weeks. The fourth-years will be leaving at the end of this week. What do you want to do? Would you like to interview the third-year juniors too?"

"No!" came the swift reply.

Dr. Applegate was taken aback. "Harold?"

"I'm sorry, Basil. Miss Emme said you would try to get me to interview third-year juniors." He offered a slight smile. "She said I should insist on only fourth-year juniors."

Dr. Applegate let out a hearty laugh. "This Miss Emme seems to know me pretty well. I should like to meet her. You will have to introduce us."

Harold sounded surprised. "You mean you don't know her? She said you were one of her favorite people!"

Dr. Applegate continued to laugh. "I am? Honestly, Harold, I do not know a Miss Emme. Where did you meet her?"

Harold became very confused. "I had lunch with her in the park across the street just a little while ago. She said she worked here at the hospital. She had an unusual way of pronouncing words. I don't think she is British. She could be Canadian," he said musingly. "She was very nice and so kind . . ."

Dr. Applegate, having regained his composure, said, "I am sure she was. Harold, at this hospital, we have over a thousand employees."

Harold said sadly, "Quite. I forgot I am not in Bellechester anymore where everyone knows everyone else."

"Now, how would you like to proceed? Should I set up an interview with Dr. Reginald Westby?"

"What I would like to do is have you admit me as a patient. I would like to test his skill and bedside manner. And I do not want him to know that I am your classmate or a doctor."

"Harold, I can't go admitting a healthy person to this hospital just so he can do a job interview. The National Health Service would be all over me. I have to account for every bed taken."

"Basil, I have thought about this long and hard," Harold replied. "I want to experience this young doctor from a patient's perspective. I figured the only way to do that would be for me to be a patient myself. Besides, at my clinic, people are always coming in with vague symptoms. Let's see how good a diagnostician he is. It has been years since I have had a good physical examina-tion anyway."

"I must say, that is quite an unusual way to conduct a physician search. But the more I think about it, the more sense it makes. All right, I will do as you wish. And I will hold your con-fidence. For the duration of your stay, you shall be Mr. Harold Merton from Bellechester." Dr. Applegate got up and walked around his desk. "I will have Mrs. Stanfield call for an orderly to take you down to admitting so you can fill out the paperwork. I'll call them and let them know you are coming. I want to make sure that your room will be on this floor. Best to get you settled straightaway so you won't miss supper. Before I leave for the evening, I'll stop in and check in on you. If Dr. Westby doesn't stop in tonight, he will see you bright and early on his rounds tomorrow morning. Good luck, Harold."

He shook Harold's hand before he opened his office door. Once in the outer office, he spoke to Mrs. Stanfield. "Mrs. Stanfield, please call for an orderly to take Dr. Merton down to admitting. Looks like he will be staying with us for a few days. Oh, and from now on, we will refer to Dr. Merton as Mr. Merton. He does not want anyone to know he is a physician. He does not want any special treatment."

"Very good, Doctor," Mrs. Stanfield replied. She picked up the phone and made the call. To Harold, she said, "It might be a few minutes. Please have a seat, Mr. Merton." She pointed to the waiting area.

"Thank you, Mrs. Stanfield." Harold went and sat down in the reception area and waited for the orderly to come.

CHAPTER 3

AN ENTERTAINING EVENING

Miss Emme had been right. From the orderly who wheeled him down to admitting and back, to the clerk who processed the paperwork, to the young nurse who got him settled into bed, everyone treated him with care and respect. Now that everyone had left him alone, Harold took stock of the surroundings that would be his home for the next few days. True to his word, Dr. Applegate had gotten him a private room on the seventh floor. The room was on the wing and faced outward. He could see rooftops and office buildings in that part of London. Only a small patch of sky was visible. Harold was already homesick for Bellechester, where there was always plenty of sky above and trees and acres of green, open spaces. Right then and there, Harold promised himself that he would never take the scenery at home for granted ever again.

There was a painting of an English garden with a small stone cottage on the wall opposite his bed. Harold found the picture comforting. That was exactly the kind of place he imagined for his retirement. The room also contained his own small bathroom and a closet that held his clothes and his suitcase. On the nightstand, he placed his prayer book, Rosary, and his new crossword puzzle book that he had purchased for himself at the Newport station while he was waiting for the London train. He also had a notebook and pencils to record his impressions of his hospital stay; a chair and a movable table that could slide over his bed rounded out the room's furnishings. Right now, he had everything he needed, except a young doctor to take back to Bellechester.

Harold was busy recording the events of the day in his notebook when Dr. Applegate stopped by on his way home. When they were in medical school together, they were inseparable. Although their lives took different paths, they still exchanged Christmas cards that included a short note each year. They had a good visit. There was lots of laughter as they reminisced about the "old days." Harold wished Basil would stay longer, but he knew he had to get home to his wife, Caroline.

Before he left, Basil told Harold, "I was not able to find Dr. Westby, so do not expect to see him until tomorrow morning. Because no orders were written for you, you can expect a quiet evening and an undisturbed night. I imagine you will want to rest up after your long journey today."

After Basil left, Harold continued writing in his journal. Supper was nourishing, but nothing like what Mrs. Duggan, his cook and housekeeper of the last fourteen years, would have made him. The carrots were overcooked and mushy. The potato was hard, and the beef was tough, although he did enjoy his custard pudding. But then, Harold always enjoyed dessert.

After his tray was taken away, the evening stretched before him. For some odd reason,

Harold kept replaying his encounter with Miss Emme in his head. He wondered whether she would be able to find him. And most disturbing of all, he wondered why it mattered so much to him that she did find him again. After all, he had just met her for a brief time. All those years he'd lived in Bellechester, his practice had kept him so busy that he'd had no time for finding a wife. He had always been very careful not to blur the lines between doctor and patient. Back in school, when Basil was dating Caroline, they had tried to set him up numerous times with blind dates, but nothing stuck. To be truthful, he was not lonely. He was the quiet type who didn't mind solitude. If he had one or two good friends for companionship, well, then, that was all he needed. His best friend in Bellechester was the pastor at the local Catholic church, Father Mathias Evenson. Their friendship ran deep and spanned decades. But at this moment, he wished his old friend were here with him. He longed to share with him the events of the day.

It was shortly after seven when there was a knock on his door. Harold called out, "Come in."

Mary Elizabeth stuck her head around the door. "Am I disturbing you?"

"No, not at all," Harold said eagerly. "Come in, please."

Mary Elizabeth came in and sat down in the chair next to his bed. "Mr. Merton, I just wanted to see how you are getting on."

"Please, call me Harold. After all, we did have lunch together."

Mary Elizabeth laughed. "So we did. All right, Harold, how has everyone been treating you?"

"Miss Emme, you were right. Everyone has been kind and helpful."

"Good. That's what I like to hear."

"I am curious. How did you ever find me?"

"Simple deduction," Mary Elizabeth said as she tapped her finger to her temple. "I know that Dr. Applegate usually puts his fourth-year juniors' patients on the seventh floor. Then I just asked at the nurses' station if there were any new admits this afternoon."

Harold laughed. "Remind me to tell you about my friend Father Evenson. He is also very good at deduction. I think you would like him."

"I'm sure I would. How did your meeting with Dr. Applegate go? Did you get your fourth-year junior doctor?"

"I did, thanks to you. You were right. He did try to get me to take a third-year, but I was firm. Luckily, I got the last one," Harold said triumphantly.

Mary Elizabeth asked, "The last one? What do you mean?"

Harold said, "Dr. Applegate assigned Dr. Westby to my case because he is the only one who does not have firm employment plans as of yet."

"I'm sorry, Harold, I'm not following you. What do employment plans have to do with anything? All of the fourth-year doctors are on staff through August twenty-eighth. Any one of the five could have been assigned to you."

For a moment, Harold wanted to tell Miss Emme the real purpose for his hospital stay. She had an amazing ability to compel him to open up and tell her everything. But he thought better of it. He had just arrived, and Basil had gone to great lengths to accommodate his wishes. He did not want to reveal his true identity just yet, so he changed the subject. "You're not from here, are you? Are you Canadian?"

"What?!" Mary Elizabeth burst out laughing. "Now who is trying to use his deductive abilities? And change the subject at the same time."

"Well, am I right?" Harold inquired.

"Yes to your first query and no to your second," Mary Elizabeth replied, still laughing.

"What kind of answer is that?" Harold exclaimed.

"A perfectly honest answer to both of your questions." Mary Elizabeth was having a hard time regaining her composure. "Yes, you are correct. I am not from around 'here,' by which, I assume, you mean Great Britain. And I am not from Canada."

"Well, then, where are you from?" Harold asked with much exasperation.

Mary Elizabeth took a moment to compose herself and said, "I am from the village of St. Ursula, Stearns County, state of Minnesota, United States of America."

"Aha!" Harold said defiantly. "American!"

"Goodness, Harold," Mary Elizabeth said. "The way you said 'American.' Being from America is not a crime."

"No, but it does explain your 'interpretation' of the English language," Harold retorted, smiling.

Mary Elizabeth feigned indignation. "I am sure that if we consulted a dictionary, you would find more than one acceptable pronunciation for a word." She paused. "I fear if we keep this up, we will be fighting the American Revolution all over again." She leaned over to him. "And you know how that turned out. So, now *I* am going to change the subject. Okay, Harold, now it's your turn."

"My turn?"

"Yes," Mary Elizabeth replied. "I told you where I am from; now you tell me where home is for you. You already told me you are not from London. Again, using my deductive powers, I have already reached two conclusions: One, I surmise you had to travel a ways to get to this hospital. And two, your hometown is not a city or even a very large town."

"Do I seem like a country bumpkin to you? Today I sure felt like one," Harold said.

"Listen, my hometown has a population of 267, so I am not about to call anyone a country bumpkin."

"But you seem so confident, so sure of yourself."

"Part of it can be attributed to supportive family and teachers. They told me I could be anything, do anything, if I put my mind to it and believed in myself. And I will tell you a secret." Mary Elizabeth motioned to him. She leaned over to Harold, and she whispered, "I am part duck."

Harold fell back on his pillows and howled in laughter. "Did you say you are part duck?!" he exclaimed.

"Shush!" Mary Elizabeth said seriously as she looked about the room. "Someone will hear you."

"Really? Part duck?" Harold, still laughing, said in a quieter tone of voice.

"Haven't you ever watched a duck swim in the water?"

"Of course, many times."

"Well, on the surface, they glide gracefully through the water like nothing fazes them, all calm and peaceful. But, if you look underneath the water"—she paused for emphasis—"their feet are paddling like . . . *heck!*" Mary Elizabeth sat back in the chair and smiled.

Harold lay back and laughed. "Oh, Miss Emme, you are too much."

"Now, back to you. I am not letting you off the hook. I really want to know. How many people live in your hometown?"

"Six hundred in the village and surrounding farms. If you add the populations of the two monasteries outside town, then eight hundred."

"Monasteries? What kind?"

"St. Gertrude's for women and St. Bede's for men. Both are Benedictine Roman Catholic."

"And the name of this village is . . ."

"Bellechester."

"See, now that wasn't so hard. Tell me more about the village," Mary Elizabeth said as she settled back in the chair.

As Harold described the village he loved, he became more animated. He painted such a vivid picture that Mary Elizabeth could imagine herself standing in the middle of the village square. She sighed. "Bellechester sounds like a beautiful place to live."

"It is. I could never imagine living anywhere else."

"For a village that size, doesn't Bellechester have a resident doctor?"

Harold answered truthfully, "Yes, we do. Unfortunately, he is getting on in years, and I just wanted someone younger to take my case. I figured my friend Dr. Applegate could set me up. So far, so good."

Mary Elizabeth replied, "I see." She looked at her watch. "It's getting late. I should be going home. You need to rest up. Morning rounds start around here at seven. You need to be in top form for Dr. Westby tomorrow."

"Can't you stay just a little longer?"

Mary Elizabeth chuckled. "I haven't heard pleading like that since I used to babysit my younger brothers and sisters."

"Did it work?"

Mary Elizabeth let out a big sigh. "Every time." She glanced at Harold's nightstand and spied the familiar beads. "Have you prayed your Rosary yet today?"

"No, not yet."

"Okay, here's the deal. We will pray the Rosary together, and after that, no more talking. Then I will leave and you will go to sleep. Agreed?"

"Agreed."

"I'm going to step out for about fifteen minutes. Will that be enough time for you to take care of your bedtime business?"

"Yes."

"Good. See you in a bit." With that, Mary Elizabeth left the room.

CHAPTER 4

Matron Carruthers

When Mary Elizabeth left Harold's room, she headed to the nurses' station at the end of the hall. Her heart sank when she saw that her least favorite nurse, Matron Carruthers, was at the desk. Tonight she was in no mood to be on the receiving end of her biting remarks.

When Matron Carruthers saw Mary Elizabeth, she scolded her. "I heard you were in the wing, Dr. Senty. You are very loud. You should not be laughing and riling up the patients. Patients are not here to be entertained. They are here to rest. They need peace and quiet! The way you behave, especially with the male patients, well, it is disgraceful. Mark my words: Dr. Applegate shall hear about your unprofessional behavior tonight. I shall make a full report."

Mary Elizabeth ignored the rebuke and counted to ten in her head. As Matron Carruthers continued, Mary Elizabeth made it all the way up to thirty-seven. A new record! When Matron Carruthers had finally finished, Mary Elizabeth calmly said, "I'd like to see the chart for Mr. Merton in room 712."

"Mr. Merton is not your patient. Dr. Applegate assigned him to Dr. Westby," Matron Carruthers sniped.

"Has Dr. Westby been in to see him tonight?"

"No, he left early again. Probably had a date. If Dr. Westby paid as much attention to his patients as he did to his love life, they would be better off."

"I will be attending Mr. Merton with Dr. Westby," Mary Elizabeth lied, "and I need to prepare for rounds tomorrow morning." Mary Elizabeth now spoke very firmly, "Now, may I please have his chart?" Mary Elizabeth usually did not tell lies. She had intended to ask Dr. Applegate if she could be assigned to Harold's case but had not gotten around to it yet. She promised herself she would ask him first thing tomorrow morning.

"Much good it will do you," Matron Carruthers said as she handed over Harold's chart.

For once, Mary Elizabeth did not take exception to the matron's remark. It was true. Harold's chart was blank except for some personal information. She noticed that under emergency contact, his friend Father Mathias Evenson was listed. Under name of primary physician, Dr. Applegate had written his own name. Attending physician was Dr. Westby. Dr. Applegate did, however, add a special note: *Dr. Westby is to perform all medical procedures on Mr. Merton.* Mary Elizabeth found that an odd note to put in his chart. After looking at it for a few minutes, Mary Elizabeth handed the chart back to Matron Carruthers. Mary Elizabeth asked, "Did Dr. Applegate give any other special instructions?"

"Besides that note, the only other instruction was that after we took away his dinner tray tonight, we were not to disturb him. Apparently," the matron said pointedly, "you did not receive that message."

Mary Elizabeth's only reply was, "No, I did not." Mary Elizabeth left the nurses' station and headed to the supply closet. She grabbed what she needed and was on her way back to Harold's room when Matron Carruthers intercepted her in the hall.

"Where do you think you are going with that?" she said, pointing at the bottle of body lotion Mary Elizabeth held in her hand.

"I am going to attend to my patient," Mary Elizabeth said calmly.

The matron's voice was stern. "Dr. Applegate explicitly gave the order that Mr. Merton was not to be disturbed."

Mary Elizabeth replied, "Dr. Applegate gave the order to the nursing staff, not to the doctors." Her tone became severe. "I expect you and your staff to abide by Dr. Applegate's order, Matron Carruthers. Is that understood?"

Matron Carruthers glared at Mary Elizabeth for a few moments. Mary Elizabeth remained firm, stood her ground, and glared back. Seeing that Dr. Senty was not going to back down, the head nurse finally mumbled, "Yes, Doctor," and walked back to the nurses' station.

When Mary Elizabeth entered room 712, Harold was still in the bathroom. Mary Elizabeth set the lotion on the table. She sank in the chair next to Harold's bed and put her hand to her head. Besides it being a long day, her encounters with Matron Carruthers always left her mentally and emotionally drained. She had told a lie, and it did bother her. *Why does Matron Carruthers always bring out the worst in me? Oh well, something else to discuss with my confessor on Saturday.*

When Harold emerged from the bathroom, Mary Elizabeth handed him the Rosary. "Here, you lead," was all she said.

Harold got himself settled in bed, and as they began to pray, they soon fell into the Rosary's familiar and soothing rhythm.

Outside Harold's room, the nosy matron had her ear to the door. A young nurse, Nurse Daly, came upon her. "Matron Carruthers, what are you doing?" she asked.

"Shh! I'm trying to hear what they are saying, but I can't make anything out. Here, you listen," the matron whispered.

Obediently, the young nurse put her ear to the door and listened. After a few moments, she straightened up.

"Well, what did you hear?" Matron Carruthers whispered.

"Matron, they are praying the Rosary together. The Joyful Mysteries, to be exact," she said.

"The Rosary!" Carruthers exclaimed.

"Yes, I saw a Rosary on Mr. Merton's nightstand when I went in to remove his dinner tray. Didn't you know? Dr. Senty is also Catholic. She often prays with her patients." With that, Nurse Daly turned and walked back to the nurses' station. After a few minutes, the matron followed her.

When they finished praying, Harold handed the Rosary to Mary Elizabeth, and she put it back on the nightstand. She got up and went into the bathroom. After washing her hands, she came and stood by the bed.

She talked softly. "The nurses were instructed to leave you alone tonight, so they will not be in to give you your nightly back rub. Would you like me to give you one? It will relax you and help you get a good night's sleep."

Mary Elizabeth spoke in such calm and even tones that Harold could only nod in agreement. When he was on his stomach, Mary Elizabeth made sure his body was aligned in the proper position. She gathered his pajama top around his neck. She squirted the lotion into her hands, spreading the lotion evenly on her palms, and began. As she worked, she could feel the tightness in his shoulder muscles. "Harold, your shoulder muscles are so tense. You will never get a good night's sleep all bound up like that."

"I am afraid you have discovered where I store all my worries," Harold said.

"Would you like me to massage your shoulder muscles to try to get some of those kinks out?" she asked.

"Do you think you can? I have lots of worries," Harold replied.

"I can't make any promises, but I will do my best for you. Now, you just close your eyes and think about your favorite place back home where you go to relax. No more worries. Just think peaceful thoughts."

"All right, Miss Emme. Let's see what you can do."

Once she was satisfied with the state of his shoulder muscles, she kept a steady movement up and down his back. After fifteen minutes, Mary Elizabeth stopped and pulled down his top and arranged the blankets over him. Her voice was now barely a whisper as she said, "Good night, Harold." As she left, she turned off his overhead room light.

CHAPTER 5

Miss Emme Makes an Impression

It was raining. Mary Elizabeth's boardinghouse was several streets from the hospital. She usually took her time walking to the hospital, as this, and her return trip home, would be her only chance to be outdoors. Growing up in the country, she tried to take in all the sights and sounds of nature on each trip. But today, she was anxious to get to the hospital. Her stride was almost a run, and her surroundings became a blur, as she was single-minded in her determination to speak to Dr. Applegate before the morning rounds began.

By the time she entered the hospital, she was out of breath. She shed her wet raincoat and headscarf in the lift. It was half-past six when Mary Elizabeth arrived on the seventh floor. She headed to the junior doctors' lounge, where she hung her wet raincoat on the small coatrack at the back of the room. Opening her locker, she pulled out her lab coat and put it on.

Dr. Ruhan Batra was already sitting at the table poring over patient charts, a cup of steaming hot tea by his side. He called out, "Good morning, Mary Elizabeth. A little English dew falling this morning."

"Morning, Ruhan. Ah yes, a little summer rain is always good for the crops. Have you seen Reggie this morning?"

"No, not yet. So far, it's just you and me. Yesterday, he was boasting about some date he was going to have with one of the nurses from the surgical ward. They were going to see a play in the West End. I don't expect to see him crawl in until later."

"Well, if you happen to see him before I do, could you tell him I want to talk to him before he starts his rounds?"

She was still speaking when Dr. Stuart Harrington III walked in the door. "Which one of us poor male doctors do you have in your sights this morning?" he asked teasingly.

"Don't worry, Stuey. It's not you . . . this time," Mary Elizabeth retorted playfully. Stuey was the good-natured one of their group who kept the atmosphere light. Over the years, Mary Elizabeth had come to think of him like a brother.

"Whew!" Dr. Harrington replied as he wiped his brow. "In that case, I shall come in and start my day. Say, who are you looking for? You know Connor has his interview at the Medical Research Council this morning, so he won't be in until the afternoon."

"I'm looking for Reggie. Oh, I do hope Connor gets the position. I have never seen anyone get as excited about petri dishes and laboratories as Connor," Mary Elizabeth said.

"Yes, definitely a match made in heaven," agreed Ruhan.

"Well, I'm off. I'll see you all later." Mary Elizabeth walked out the door and down the hall to Dr. Applegate's office. Since Mrs. Stanfield did not start work until half-past eight, Mary Elizabeth walked right into the outer office. She could see Dr. Applegate at his desk and so knocked on the open door.

"Come in," came the answer.

"Dr. Applegate? Could I speak to you for a few minutes?"

"Of course, Dr. Senty. Have a seat," he said as he pointed to the chair in front of his desk. "What can I do for you?"

"I know you have a rule about junior doctors not caring for more than four patients at a time, but I might be discharging one of mine today, and I was wondering if I could team up with Dr. Westby to attend one of his patients?"

"Any patient, or is there one in particular?" Dr. Applegate had an amused look on his face. He sat back in his office chair and smiled.

Mary Elizabeth could feel herself blushing. "There was a new admit to the floor yesterday, a Mr. Merton in 712."

"Ah yes, Mr. Merton. May I ask, why the interest in Mr. Merton?" Dr. Applegate seemed to be enjoying questioning Mary Elizabeth.

Mary Elizabeth learned a long time ago that it was best to just come right out and say what was on her mind. She took a deep breath and said, "Two reasons. One is that I happened to see his chart last night and it was blank. I think it would be a good challenge to see what I could do for him. Second, coming from a small town, I know how overwhelming a large city like London can be. He just seems like a lost soul, and I thought I could help him feel more comfortable while he is staying with us."

Dr. Applegate sat forward and clasped his hands together on the desk, looking Mary Elizabeth straight in the eye. "Thank you for being frank with me. I have always appreciated your directness and your honesty. Not to change the subject, but do you know what was waiting for me on my desk this morning?"

Mary Elizabeth gave out a large sigh and rolled her eyes. "Might it have been a tome from Matron Carruthers? I don't think she could have possibly written all the ways I disgraced the medical profession last night in just a note."

Dr. Applegate tried to be serious, but he burst out laughing. Then, regaining his composure, he said, "Matron Carruthers is a competent nurse and an experienced supervisor. As you are painfully aware, she has taken it upon herself to mold not only her nurses but also you young doctors. In her note to me this morning, she did lay out some serious concerns against you, Dr. Senty. But I try to be fair and hear all sides, so I went to see Mr. Merton first thing this morning to get his impressions of last night."

"And?" Mary Elizabeth asked as she moved closer to the edge of her chair.

"Funny thing," he said after a long pause. "Mr. Merton swears he never met a Dr. Senty."

"Oh?"

"Indeed. So, that means I do not have to address the matron's concerns with you, except to say, please exercise more discretion in your dealings with patients. Matron Carruthers does have at least one valid point among the many."

"Yes, Dr. Applegate," Mary Elizabeth said contritely.

Dr. Applegate continued, "Even though he did not know a Dr. Senty, Mr. Merton did go on and on for quite some time about a Miss Emme. Apparently, her visit last night was just what he needed. It raised his spirits and kept him from dwelling on his worries. He also said that the back rub she gave him helped him sleep soundly through the night. He reported that it was the best night's sleep he has had in years. So if you happen to run into Miss Emme, please tell her that she made a positive impression on one of our patients last night. You see, healing is not always about pills and procedures. Healing can take place on many levels. A good doctor knows that instinctively."

Then he sat back in his chair and smiled. "I do believe Miss Emme would make"—he paused and looked directly at her with his sparkling blue eyes — "or shall I say, Miss Emme *is becoming* a very good doctor."

Mary Elizabeth was relieved. "Thank you, Dr. Applegate." She paused and then, smiling, said,

"If I see Miss Emme, I will be sure to pass along your message to her."

"Someday," Dr. Applegate said with a twinkle in his eyes, "I shall like to meet Miss Emme. And I do hope that Miss Emme will continue to visit Mr. Merton. Her visits do a world of good for him."

Dr. Applegate sat back up in his chair and was all business again. "Now, with that being said, I am going to respond to your initial request. For now, I would like Dr. Westby to care for Mr. Merton alone. But I will put you down as co-attending physician so you will be able to legally access Mr. Merton's chart and follow his progress. That way, you should have no trouble from Matron Carruthers. I know that is not the answer you wanted to hear, but please, believe me, I do have my reasons for doing things this way for now. Know that I have Mr. Merton's best interest in mind. You will just have to trust me."

"Yes, of course, Dr. Applegate. I do trust you. Thank you for hearing me out." With that, Mary Elizabeth stood up. "Oh, and just so you know," she said, with her characteristic smile, "Miss

Emme will be pleased to continue her visits with Mr. Merton." She turned and left the office to begin her morning rounds. As she walked away, she could hear Dr. Applegate chuckling.

CHAPTER 6

MORNING ROUNDS

Mary Elizabeth's first patient of the day was Mrs. Plinkton. She was a hearty, salt-of-the-earth type in her forties, married, and the mother of six children. She'd had her gallbladder removed seven days earlier.

After examining her, Mary Elizabeth said, "You are doing wonderfully, Mrs. Plinkton. Your incision is healing nicely, and there are no signs of infection. Your test results are all within the normal range. How do you feel about the prospect of going home today?"

Mrs. Plinkton said, "I am anxious to get back home. Goodness knows what the house looks like after me being gone so long. I confess, I do miss my husband and children."

Mary Elizabeth reminded her, "Remember what we talked about yesterday. You just had major surgery. Housework and caring for children are very demanding tasks. You are restricted in what you can do and especially what you can lift and carry for the next month. Now, have you discussed things with your husband, or would you like me to speak with him?"

"My husband, Bert, is a good man, make no mistake. But I think it would be best if he heard those instructions from you, if it's not too much trouble."

"Not at all. Maybe he could also bring one of your older children too, when he comes to pick you up. Do you have a child over twelve?" Mary Elizabeth asked.

Mrs. Plinkton laughed. "Oh, Dr. Senty. You flatter me, thinking I'm a young mother. The youngest is seven, then eight, ten, twelve, fifteen, and seventeen."

Mary Elizabeth said, "In that case, have him bring the two oldest. I would love to meet them. I am also asking a dietitian to come and join our party. There are some dietary restrictions to discuss, foods you should not be eating as well as foods that will aid in your recovery. What time do you think they will be able to pick you up today?"

"Bert works until five-thirty. I don't think they could make it until after seven tonight. That would make an awfully long day for you, Dr. Senty."

"Not to worry. That will give me time to have some written instructions ready for you to take home. Now, I will alert the nursing staff to get you all cleaned up and ready to go home. Be sure they give you access to a phone so you can call your husband to arrange for your departure. The nurses will also take you on a walk a couple of times today. The rest of the day will be yours to rest up. Do you have any questions for me?"

"No, you've explained everything very well."

"All right, until tonight, then. You have a good day."

Mrs. Plinkton took Mary Elizabeth's hand. "Thank you for everything."

After leaving her room, Mary Elizabeth went down to the junior doctors' lounge and wrote down her notes in Mrs. Plinkton's chart. Then she went to the nurses' station and gave instructions to Matron Hartly. After receiving the chart for her next patient, Mary Elizabeth asked, "Is Dr. Westby on the floor this morning?"

Matron Hartly answered, "I have not seen him today. Could he be off on an interview?"

Mary Elizabeth replied, "He never said anything about an interview. And as far as I know, he was not scheduled to be in surgery this morning. If you do see him, please tell him I would like to see him before he sees Mr. Merton in 712." Mary Elizabeth checked her watch. It read 7:36 a.m. "Has Mr. Merton gotten breakfast this morning?"

"No. The trays have not come up yet."

"Hold his breakfast until either Dr. Westby or I have seen him this morning and done our intake assessment."

"Yes, Doctor. Mr. Merton must be a VIP with all the attention he is getting from Dr. Applegate and you. Dr. Applegate saw him first thing this morning, and then he was back again a short while ago to write in his chart. He told us that you would also be attending him. Would you like to see his chart?"

"Yes, thank you." Mary Elizabeth took the chart. True to his word, Dr. Applegate had also written Dr. Senty's name in the attending physician space. No notes from Dr. Westby. Mary Elizabeth was torn. She did not want to interfere, but she also did not want Mr. Merton to go without breakfast either. Mary Elizabeth gave the chart back to Matron Hartly. She said, "It really is Dr. Westby's call as to how he wants to proceed. But he is not here yet. So here is what we will do. If Dr. Westby does not see him by eight-thirty, then please find me. I know it will be a late breakfast for Mr. Merton, but at least he will get something. I will check back with you in between patients this morning."

"Yes, Doctor."

Mary Elizabeth continued her rounds. Mr. Thornbury was being treated for bacterial pneumonia. His case was particularly complicated, as he also was a diabetic and a heavy smoker. He was receiving antibiotics and was in an oxygen tent. After two days, there had been only a slight improvement. After examining him, Mary Elizabeth decided to continue with the treatment. It was very difficult for him to breathe, much less talk. Mary Elizabeth held his hand and told him that they were doing everything they could for him. He gave her a slight nod and squeezed her hand to let her know he heard and understood her. Mary Elizabeth gave him a smile and told him to rest. As she left his room, she hoped that he had not seen how worried she truly was about his condition. When she returned his chart to the nurses' station, she again checked Mr. Merton's chart. Still no sighting of Dr. Westby on the floor.

Mary Elizabeth checked in on Miss Atkinson, who was undergoing tests for her severe headaches. Mary Elizabeth spent time with her explaining the tests scheduled for her. Dr. Senty said she would share the test results with her as soon as they were available. She also reassured Miss Atkinson that she was consulting with the neurologists on staff. She spent some time visiting with Miss Atkinson and discovered that she had been a librarian for many years. They had a long chat discussing their favorite books and authors.

Her last patient of the morning was a young college student, Ronald Baxter. He had been in a motorcycle accident, had broken his leg in several places, and had suffered multiple scrapes and scratches. After several days, his condition had stabilized. The swelling had gone down on his broken leg, so he was scheduled for surgery that afternoon. Mary Elizabeth was going to operate with the senior orthopedic specialist assisting. Mary Elizabeth wanted to be sure he knew what was going to happen, so she took him step-by-step through the procedure. She was impressed by his interest in the surgery and the depth of the questions he asked. She reassured him that she would be there when he awoke from the anesthesia and would let him know how the surgery went.

CHAPTER 7

DR. WESTBY MAKES AN APPEARANCE

After finishing with her morning rounds, Mary Elizabeth worked on her charting in the junior doctors' lounge. Ruhan and Stuey were also working on their charts. It was after eight-fifteen when Dr. Reginald Westby finally walked into the room. He wore dark sunglasses even though it was raining. As usual, he looked like he had just stepped out of a gentleman's magazine. Tall, with boyish good looks and sandy-blond hair that he wore parted on the side with bangs slicked back like a movie star. No wonder all the nurses, young and even not-so-young, referred to him as *Dr. Star.*

For a tall man, Reginald Westby carried himself with an air of grace and self-assurance. Stuey looked up and said, "The prodigal returns. Glad you could join us."

After putting on his white coat, he poured himself a cup of tea and joined everyone at the table. "Last night, I saw my future unfold right in front of me," Reggie said.

"Man, that must have been some play," Ruhan said.

Now that he had everyone's attention, Reggie continued, "The play was the usual Oscar Wilde farce. Quite funny and entertaining, but the best part was—"

"Let me guess," Stuey interrupted. "The best part was after the play with Nurse Whatever-the-Flavor-of-the-Week-Is."

Reggie answered with a sly grin, "Yes, that too, but"—giving a nod in Mary Elizabeth's direction—"I will tell you blokes later."

Mary Elizabeth piped up, "Oh, thank goodness. Spare me all the sordid details."

Reggie ignored her. "The best part was running into Dr. Sims during intermission."

"Dr. Sims, head of St. Luke's Hospital?" Ruhan asked.

"The very same. We got to talking, and I told him about my interest in hospital administration. He invited my date and me to join him and his wife for dessert after the play. Turns out, he has a lower-level position open on his staff. He wants me to call his office today to set up a time for an interview," Reggie said as he put his hands behind his head and lazily stretched his lanky frame out on his chair.

"Earth to Reggie. Before you zoom into the future, how about you get your act together and concentrate on the present? You got a new admit yesterday, a Mr. Merton in 712, and the nurses are holding up the poor man's breakfast waiting for your orders. You need to do the intake," Mary Elizabeth said.

"I'll get the nurses to do it," Reggie said, unconcerned. "Why do you care?"

"Haven't you even looked at his chart?" Mary Elizabeth asked.

"How could I?" Reggie said. "I just got in."

Mary Elizabeth was getting upset. "Well, let me give you the highlights. Dr. Applegate assigned him to you yesterday afternoon. He specifically wrote that you are to perform all medical procedures on him, and that includes doing the initial evaluation."

"Okay, Mother!" Reggie answered sarcastically. "Say, how do you know so much? Did you peek at his chart? Naughty, naughty!"

"Better be careful, Mary Elizabeth, or Reggie here will tell your best friend, Matron Carruthers," Stuey warned.

"Oh, honestly!" Mary Elizabeth exclaimed. "Dr. Applegate put me down as co-attending physician, and I don't want Reggie mucking things up."

"Afraid I am going to tarnish your otherwise pristine, all-American reputation?" Reggie teased.

Mary Elizabeth just put her head down and returned to her charts. She dismissed him with a wave of her hand as if she were shooing away a pesky fly.

"Aha!" Reggie cried. "I knew it! You're jealous! You're upset because Dr. Applegate assigned him to me instead of you. Really, Mary Elizabeth, that shade of green does not look good on you."

"Well, Reggie," said Ruhan, glancing at his watch, "you can ask Dr. Applegate yourself why she was also assigned to your patient in about thirty-five minutes when he comes in for morning conferences. I am sure he'll be looking for you to give us all a full report on your new patient."

Ruhan's remark wiped the self-satisfied grin right off Reggie's face. "Yes, well, I'd best be going." Reggie scrambled up and out the door.

After Reggie left the room, Mary Elizabeth turned to Ruhan and said, "Thanks, Ruhan."

"Reggie is a fool. I hope he gets that job in administration," Ruhan said.

"At least the patients will be safer," Stuey added.

"This is true," Mary Elizabeth replied, and everyone went back to their charting.

CHAPTER 8

ℰMME TO THE RESCUE

Mary Elizabeth finished her charting and got up to pour herself a cup of tea. She put the steaming cup down at her place. She looked at her watch. There were still a good ten minutes before the morning conference started. She decided to go out and walk the halls to stretch her legs while her tea cooled down. She walked past the nurses' station and down the other wing, all the way to the end of the hallway, where there was a large window from which she could look down into the center courtyard. It was her favorite view, as she could see the flowers and the fountain.

Even in the rain, the fountain was still flowing. She lingered at the window for several minutes. Looking at her watch again, she saw it was time to head back to the junior doctors' lounge. She would just have time to gather her charts and pick up her tea. The conference room was right next door, so there would still be time to get settled before Dr. Applegate convened the morning gathering. As she walked past the nurses' station, she noticed there was no one at the desk.

She was collecting her things and settling into her place when Dr. Applegate walked into the conference room. Looking around the room, he said to Mary Elizabeth, "Where is the rest of your cohort this morning?"

Mary Elizabeth said in a surprised tone of voice, "I honestly don't know. Drs. Batra and Harrington were in the lounge just a few minutes ago. Dr. Westby was in with Mr. Merton."

As she was still speaking, the three doctors came into the room. All of them looked rumpled and disheveled as they carried in their charts and teacups. Their shirttails had come untucked from their trousers. Their hair was tousled, and all three looked like they were on the losing end of a rugby scrum.

Dr. Westby could be heard saying, "Thanks, guys. I could not have gotten him settled without you."

Once everyone was seated, Dr. Applegate said, "Now that everyone is here, shall we begin? Dr. Westby, you look like you have a story to tell. Why don't we start with you? Give us an update on your patients. Why don't you begin with your new patient, in room 712?"

Dr. Westby began, "The patient is a sixty-one-year-old male who was admitted yesterday afternoon. He came in with vague complaints of not feeling well. He talked about not being able to sleep, being anxious about the future, and always being tired. His temperature was normal. Blood pressure was a little low, ninety over sixty-three. The oral interview went fine, but as I began to examine him, he became more agitated. He complained that my stethoscope was too cold, the blood pressure cuff was too tight, and that I wasn't taking his blood pressure correctly. He willingly gave a urine sample, but when I tried to do a blood-draw, he began to yell that I was hurting him and that I was using the wrong gauge needle and that I was going in too high to pierce the vein. My first attempt was unsuccessful, and as I began to try again, he grabbed the needle from me and attempted to do it himself. That is when I left the room and called for assistance from Drs. Harrington and Batra. I administered a five-milligram injection of diazepam. He then settled down, but for everyone's safety, I instructed the nurses to secure him in his bed."

Mary Elizabeth shot up and cried, "*You restrained and sedated him?*" Immediately, she ran out of the room, down the hall, and into room 712. There she found Harold, strapped to his bed. He looked miserable. The drug was just beginning to take effect. She stood over his bed and said, "Harold, it's Emme. Don't worry. Everything is going to be all right. I'm here now."

When he heard her voice, he turned his head and looked at her with the saddest brown eyes she had ever seen. He tried to talk, but his speech was starting to slur.

It broke Mary Elizabeth's heart to see him like this. She continued to talk to him in calm tones while she began unfastening the restraints. By this time, Dr. Applegate had come into the room. He stood in the doorway and watched as Mary Elizabeth tended to his friend.

Mary Elizabeth finally removed all the straps off him. She pulled the chair over and held his hand. She kept telling him, "It's Emme. I'm here now. Everything will be all right. I won't let anyone harm you. You rest now. I will stay with you until you fall asleep. That's right. Close your eyes. I am right here." She stayed with him as he succumbed to sleep. Dr. Applegate came up and put his hand on her shoulder and motioned for her to follow him out into the hall. He led her to the conference room. By now, the room had cleared. He motioned for her to sit down. He took her teacup and went next door.

Mary Elizabeth used the time he was gone to compose herself. It was not an easy thing to do. It would take a long time to get the image of Harold strapped down in his bed with his sad, pleading eyes out of her head.

Dr. Applegate returned a few minutes later with a fresh cup of tea for them both. He sat down across from Mary Elizabeth and gently asked her, "Dr. Senty, how are you doing?"

Tears filled Mary Elizabeth's eyes again as she said, "Oh, Dr. Applegate, I let Harold—I mean Mr. Merton—down. I should have accompanied Dr. Westby this morning when he did Mr. Merton's intake and preliminary exam. Maybe I could have prevented things from escalating to the point that they did."

Dr. Applegate spoke to her gently. "Dr. Senty, listen to me. You are not to waste any more time second-guessing yourself. As doctors, we do our best, and then we have to move on because there are always other patients depending on us to do our best for them. Mr. Merton was not your patient. I assigned him to Dr. Westby. That was my decision. And I alone have to live with the consequences. Do you understand?"

"Yes, Dr. Applegate," Mary Elizabeth replied, nodding.

Dr. Applegate continued, "And it is not your job to supervise Dr. Westby or any of the other

junior doctors in your cohort. That is also my job."
He gave Mary Elizabeth a slight smile. "Now I
understand why your fellow junior doctors gave
you the nickname 'Mother.' I must say, it is well
deserved, Dr. Senty."

Mary Elizabeth gave a faint smile and sipped
her tea.

"Now, tell me, what does your schedule look
like for today, Dr. Senty?"

Mary Elizabeth ran through her schedule, including the orthopedic surgery for Mr. Baxter at
one that afternoon, the review of test results and
consult with the neurologists on Miss Atkinson,
and the family discharge conference with Mrs.
Plinkton. Mary Elizabeth also wanted to check
in and monitor the progress of Mr. Thornbury
several times during the day. She was very concerned about his lack of progress.

Dr. Applegate listened carefully. When she
finished, he said, "It looks as though today is a
particularly heavy day for you."

Mary Elizabeth said with her characteristic
bluntness, "Yes, it is. But I believe it is still manage-
able. I am only consulting with the neurologists.

They will be doing the actual testing. And in the case of Mrs. Plinkton, I have already written down most of her discharge instructions. I invited a dietitian to join us for the family conference. That conference is scheduled for seven this evening. The dietitian will be doing the bulk of the instructing tonight."

"Very wise. A doctor should know when to delegate and ask for help. Do you remember when I said that doctors do not have the luxury of second-guessing themselves?"

"Yes."

"Please remember that, because it is true. But doctors also need to be flexible and be willing to change or even reverse course when the facts present themselves. So, that is why I have decided to remove Dr. Westby from Mr. Merton's case. This morning, you have proved to me that there is only one doctor in this hospital who should be caring for Mr. Merton, and that doctor is you."

"Thank you, Dr. Applegate. I will do my very best for him," Mary Elizabeth said.

"I know you will. Mr. Merton is a very special case, and so that is why my order still stands that you perform all medical procedures on him."

"It will be my pleasure to attend to him. But I am concerned that Mr. Merton will be regaining consciousness about the time I will be in surgery. I was hoping that he would see a familiar face when he awakes."

"Don't worry, he will. I plan to be there when he comes around. I want to personally tell him about the change in his doctor. We also have other matters to discuss."

"Thank you, Dr. Applegate. That is a big relief to me."

"Good. After you are out of surgery, come to my office. We will both go to Mr. Merton, and I will introduce you to him. But I am afraid you will have to explain about Miss Emme," he said, raising his right eyebrow.

Mary Elizabeth blushed. "I do hope he won't be too disappointed to learn that I am a doctor. Please, believe me, I never meant to deceive him."

"I believe you. As I know my old friend quite well, I can say with firm assurance that Mr.

Merton will be quite pleased with the revelation that you will now be his doctor."

"I hope you are correct, Dr. Applegate."

"Now, how do you feel? Do you think you can continue on with your busy day?"

"Yes, thank you. I do feel much better after talking to you. And yes, I will be able to focus on each of my tasks for the day. I appreciate all your good advice."

"And in the interest of all parties concerned," Dr. Applegate said with a smile, "I am going to talk with Matron Carruthers this afternoon. She should not give you any trouble tonight. I do not need any extra reading material waiting for me on my desk tomorrow morning."

Unable to help herself, Mary Elizabeth let out a hearty laugh.

Dr. Applegate got up from his chair. "Before I leave you, there is one thing I haven't been able to figure out. How did you come up with that name?"

"You mean Miss Emme?"

"Yes."

"Emme is my nickname. If you take the initials from my first name, Mary Elizabeth, you get M.E. If you say them really fast, you get 'Emme.' All my family and friends back home call me by that name."

Dr. Applegate shook his head and chuckled to himself as he left the room.

CHAPTER 9

*A*N UPSETTING AFTERNOON

That afternoon, Mr. Baxter's surgery proved to be more complicated than expected, so it was almost four o'clock before Mary Elizabeth made her way to Dr. Applegate's office. As she walked in the door, Mrs. Stanfield greeted her. "Hello, Dr. Senty. Dr. Applegate asked if you could meet him in Mr. Merton's room. He also requested that it be Miss Emme who walks through the door. He said you would know what that meant."

Mary Elizabeth smiled. "Yes, that makes perfect sense to me."

"Oh, before I forget, there was a long-distance phone call for you earlier, a Dr. Richardson from Boston, Massachusetts. Because you were unavailable, he spoke to Dr. Applegate. And this letter also came for you." As she got up from her desk, she gave Mary Elizabeth a very official-looking letter that was sitting on the corner of the desk. Mrs. Stanfield said, "You are very popular today, Dr. Senty."

Mary Elizabeth took the letter and saw that it was from Newtown Hospital. She put it in the pocket of her lab coat and walked down the hall. She stopped off at the junior doctors' lounge long enough to take off her coat. She knocked on the door of room 712. Inside, she could hear Dr. Applegate and Mr. Merton having a heated discussion, so she knocked louder and walked in.

She knew that she would have to raise her voice to be heard, so she called out, "Hello, Harold. How are you doing this afternoon?" As soon as the men heard her voice, the argument stopped.

"Miss Emme!" he said. "Miss Emme, I would like you to meet my friend, Dr. Basil Applegate."

Mary Elizabeth walked over to Dr. Applegate and said, "I have seen you around the hospital. Very nice to make your acquaintance." She held out her hand.

Harold turned to Dr. Applegate and said, "Basil, this is Miss Emme."

Dr. Applegate took her hand and said, "Miss Emme, a pleasure to finally meet you. Harold has told me wonderful things about you."

Mary Elizabeth saw that Harold was dressed in his street clothes. His open suitcase lay on the bed. It was almost full. She turned to Harold and inquired, "Are you leaving us already?"

Before Harold could answer, Dr. Applegate said to Mary Elizabeth, "I am hoping you can talk him into staying. It would be a shame for him to leave now. He has not accomplished what he came here to do. As his friend and even as his doctor, I have not been able to convince him to stay."

Harold spoke very determinedly. "No, I must go. It was a mistake for me to come here. I should have never left Bellechester. I don't belong here. I must go home."

Mary Elizabeth put her hands on her hips and spoke in a stern, loud voice. "Harold Merton, you unpack that suitcase this minute. I am not going to let you leave. Yesterday, in the park, you invited me to lunch, and I will be"—her face was getting redder as she stopped and searched for an acceptable word—"d-d-d . . . darned if I am going to let you wriggle out of your promise."

Both Harold and Dr. Applegate were taken aback at the forcefulness of her remark. The room went deadly silent.

Mary Elizabeth let her words soak in for a moment. Then she smiled and said in a softer tone, "Remember, you did promise to take me to lunch. I have been looking forward to it."

Dr. Applegate said with surprise in his voice, "Harold, is that true?"

"Yes, I did promise her lunch," Harold admitted.

"Well, Mr. Harold Merton of Bellechester, are you a man of your word?" Mary Elizabeth demanded.

Harold thought for a moment. Finally, he said with conviction, "Yes, yes, I am."

A very relieved Dr. Applegate said, "Well, I guess that settles it."

Then, in her typical tone of voice, Mary Elizabeth said, "I think I have a solution where everyone will get what they want. Would you like to hear it?"

Both Harold and Dr. Applegate nodded and answered, "Yes."

Mary Elizabeth began, "Harold, I know that this morning you had a very unpleasant experience with Dr. Westby. But what I told you still holds true. There are some very good doctors in that fourth-year cohort. How about if Dr. Applegate and I put our heads together and choose another one for you? Being your primary physician, Dr. Applegate is, I'm sure, very concerned that you go through with your physical examination."

Turning to Dr. Applegate, she asked, "Isn't that right, Dr. Applegate?"

"Yes. Yes, that is quite true, Miss Emme," Dr. Applegate responded.

Turning back to Harold, Mary Elizabeth continued, "That would mean you would spend another night in the hospital. Now, I have a meeting this evening at seven, but after it is over, I promise to come and visit you. Tomorrow morning at rounds, Dr. Applegate will introduce you to your new doctor. After your physical is complete and all your tests are taken, we can have an early lunch. Depending upon the train schedule, you could even be back home in Bellechester by tomorrow evening. Now, how does that sound? Would that be acceptable?"

Before Harold could reply, Dr. Applegate interjected, "That sounds good to me, except that Caroline would never forgive me if I didn't bring you home for dinner tomorrow evening. We still have a lot of catching up to do. We were hoping you would spend the night with us. We would love to have you. Caroline could drive you to the train station on Thursday morning."

Harold listened to all that Mary Elizabeth and Basil had to say. Finally, it was his turn to speak. He said, "Miss Emme, I do want to take you to lunch tomorrow. As long as the new doctor is not one of the three I saw this morning, then yes, I will go through with my physical examination. I trust that you and Basil will choose a competent doctor for me."

Turning to Dr. Applegate, he said, "And, Basil, I would love to see dear Caroline again, so I accept your kind invitation to dinner." Now speaking with conviction in his voice, he added, "All that being said, yes, I will stay until tomorrow. Miss Emme, I think you have come up with a very good plan."

"Good!" Mary Elizabeth said. "Harold, I will let you unpack, and I will see you tonight at about eight."

"Here, Miss Emme," Dr. Applegate said, "let me walk out with you. Harold, I will stop in again before I go home."

"All right. I will see you both later," Harold said as he began to unpack his suitcase.

As they started to walk down the corridor together, Dr. Applegate said, "Thank you for getting Harold to stay. I know that he would not be happy with himself if he left now. For his sake, he needs to see this through. Now, can you come back to my office with me? I want to tell you about the phone call I received from a Dr. Richardson. And Mrs. Stanfield has a letter for you."

Mary Elizabeth said, "Yes, I picked up the letter before I saw Mr. Merton, but I have not yet had a chance to read it."

Dr. Applegate then made this unusual request: "If you could, please do not read the letter until we speak. I do believe that the phone call and the letter are related." He reassured her with a smile and said, "Now, don't worry, all will be well."

"I wasn't worried," Mary Elizabeth replied, "until now. However, I shall do as you ask. The letter is in the pocket of my lab coat, which I left in the lounge. Let me stop there first. I shall meet you in your office in a few minutes."

When Mary Elizabeth walked into the junior doctors' lounge, she saw Dr. Connor Ramsey sitting at the table working on his charts. As usual, he was so engrossed in his work, he did not even raise his head to see who entered.

"Hi, Connor. How did your interview go this morning?"

Connor looked up with a wide grin on his face. "They offered me the position. I start next week, the first of September."

"Oh, Connor, that is wonderful. Have you told the others? We must go out and celebrate!"

"That would be wonderful. Everyone knows now except Reggie. Have you seen him?"

"Not since this morning, I'm afraid. I was in surgery all afternoon. It has been a busy day. I am just here to pick up my lab coat. I am on my way to Dr. Applegate's office."

Mary Elizabeth slipped on her lab coat and proceeded down the hall to Dr. Applegate's office. Opening the outer door, she noticed that Mrs. Stanfield had already left for the day. Dr. Applegate's door was open. She knocked.

"Come in, Dr. Senty," Dr. Applegate said. "Please sit down. Can I get you anything?"

"No, thank you. I'm fine," said Mary Elizabeth as she settled into the chair in front of his desk.

"Did you bring your letter with you?" he asked.

Mary Elizabeth pulled the letter from her pocket. "Yes, it's right here."

"Before you open it, I want to tell you two things. First, and most important, I want you to believe me when I say that I am certain everything is going to work out. I know you may want to ask me more questions about that, but at this time, I can say no more. And the second thing I want to say is that over the past four years, I have watched you develop into a very fine doctor. You will do well wherever you go."

"Thank you, Dr. Applegate." Mary Elizabeth was confused by his words.

"Now to the difficult part," Dr. Applegate said sadly. "You can open your letter now. I do hope Dr. Richardson explains it better than I can, because frankly, I don't understand it at all."

Mary Elizabeth opened the letter. As she started to read, her hand went up instinctively to cover her mouth. She wanted to cry out, but she could make no sound. The letter read:

Dr. Carl Richardson, Dir. of Geriatrics
Newtown Hospital
1600 Adams Avenue
Boston, Massachusetts

August 18, 1959

Dr. Mary Elizabeth Senty
Mother of Mercy Hospital
6800 Mercy Street
London, England

Dear Dr. Senty:

It is with much regret that I inform you that I must rescind the offer to you of a post-residency fellowship for the year 1959/1960. While your academic record and recommendations are outstanding, an unfortunate incident involving you and a highly reputed member of our medical profession has come to light. Because of that incident, several of our senior doctors do not feel comfortable working with you in a collaborative setting. Newtown Hospital enjoys a reputation of being a leader in geriatric medicine, and I do not want to do anything that would endanger the good name of our doctors or this hospital.

I hope that this decision will not cause too much of a disruption in your plans. Even though we cannot offer you the fellowship, I am confident that a doctor of your skill should not have difficulty securing an appointment with another medical institution. I wish you all the best in your career.

Sincerely,

Carl Richardson, M.D., Ph.D.

As Mary Elizabeth finished the letter, she put it down in her lap.

Dr. Applegate said softly, "I am so sorry, Dr. Senty. I know how much you were looking forward to going back to the United States. Dr. Richardson called today to make sure you received his letter before you purchased your plane ticket." Dr. Applegate watched helplessly as all the life seemed to drain out of Mary Elizabeth.

"That was good of him, I suppose," Mary Elizabeth said quietly. She stood up. Then her voice became stronger, as she could no longer hold in her anger and frustration. "You know, Dr. Applegate, what hurts the most is that Elizabeth Blackwell earned her medical degree in 1849. She faced all sorts of discrimination for being a woman in a man's profession. I received my medical degree over a hundred years later, in 1954. It was not given to me; I earned it. I did everything asked of me, and more. And still, nothing has changed! Why am I still not accepted as an equal? And why is it always my fault when I am preyed upon and attacked by male doctors for their sport? What do I have to do to prove to the medical establishment that I deserve to practice medicine alongside them?"

Dr. Applegate also rose from his chair. "I am so sorry, Dr. Senty. I wish I could give you some answers to your questions, but I cannot. I regret that they are so narrow-minded. Truly, they are the ones who have lost the opportunity to benefit from your medical skill and knowledge. You have every right to be upset and angry, but you must not give up."

He paused for a moment and then continued, "I have not been blind these past four years. I have seen how patients, nurses like Matron Carruthers, and even, I am ashamed to say, some doctors at this hospital have treated you. But you have always handled yourself with dignity, grace, and humor. I wish that I could say that you are never going to run into this kind of prejudice again, but we both know that you will probably experience rejection again and again because you are a woman. But, Dr. Senty, you have to persevere. That is what is going to change the medical profession. You are going to change the medical profession."

"How can I do that when I don't have any-where to practice medicine?" Mary Elizabeth looked at him as tears began to fall. She quick-ly brushed them aside, took a deep breath, and stood tall. Her voice became controlled again as she said, "I am sorry. I didn't mean to dump all my frustration on you. You have always support-ed and believed in me. I will be forever grateful. I don't expect you to fix my problem." She stuffed the letter into her pocket. "Thank you, Dr. Ap-plegate. I should go. I don't want to take up any more of your time."

"Dr. Senty, what are you going to do now?"

"Besides attending Mrs. Plinkton's family con-ference and visiting Mr. Merton, I guess I will be busy trying to come up with an alternative plan for my future. Good night, Dr. Applegate."

Dr. Applegate stopped her. "Please, don't spend any time on making future plans tonight. After you visit with Mr. Merton, go home and get a good night's sleep. You have had an extraor-dinarily busy day today. You must be exhausted. No one can think clearly when they are that tired.

I promise you, your situation will look much different tomorrow."

As Mary Elizabeth turned to go, Dr. Applegate called out to her, "Wait. Just a minute." He sat back down at his desk and opened the middle drawer, pulling out a small notebook. "I do believe I have just the quote to leave you with tonight."

Mary Elizabeth stopped. Dr. Applegate was paging through his notebook when his finger stopped along the searched-for line and he said, "Ah yes, here it is." He cleared his throat and began, "What is it that your grandfather used to tell you? 'Even if the night sky is cloudy and all is dark, know that the stars and the moon are still there to guide you. You just have to wait until the clouds roll on by.'"

Hearing her grandfather's words spoken to her made her sit back down. Mary Elizabeth was incredulous. "You kept a record of my grandfather's sayings?"

Dr. Applegate smiled. "After hearing his sayings for over four years, this entire notebook is filled with them. From very early on, I realized that your grandfather is a very wise man. His insights into the human condition rival that of any psychologists' lectures I have ever heard. I did not want to forget any of his pearls of wisdom, so I wrote them all down. I must say, these sayings have come in handy on numerous occasions."

"Thank you, Dr. Applegate. You do my grandfather a great honor." Mary Elizabeth gave a slight smile.

Dr. Applegate said, "Now there is that Senty resiliency I have seen so often through the years. Remember, the forecast for tomorrow morning is clear with sunny skies. Before you continue on with your day, I want you to go down to the cafeteria and get something to eat. Take a break. I do not want to see you on the floor for at least one hour."

"Yes, Dr. Applegate. Thank you so much."

CHAPTER 10

NOTHING MORE TO BE DONE

On her way to the cafeteria, Mary Elizabeth stopped in the lounge to get her pocketbook. Dr. Connor Ramsey was still poring over his charts.

"Still at it, Connor?" Mary Elizabeth asked.

"I'm just about done."

"Would you like to grab a bite to eat in the cafeteria with me? I'd like to hear all about your interview."

Connor was the quietest person in their group. He was amazingly perceptive and a very good listener. "The cafeteria? Why don't we go out?" he asked.

"I'd love to get out of this place for a while, but I have a family discharge conference at seven tonight."

"Long day?"

"Yes, very."

"In that case, the cafeteria will be fine. Then maybe you can tell me what's going on around here. What did I miss this morning? Ruhan and Stuey were very subdued this afternoon. Neither wanted to talk about it. Something is going on. I am hoping you can fill me in. Why don't you go on ahead, and I'll join you shortly."

"Sounds good." She left the lounge and headed to the nurses' station to tell them she was going off the floor.

Mary Elizabeth and Connor had a pleasant dinner together. She told him all about the events of the morning.

"Reggie had better watch it. An unsatisfactory recommendation from Dr. Applegate can hurt his chances of finding a good position. Thanks for telling me. That also explains why Ruhan and Stuey didn't want to talk about it. Do you think they got in trouble too?"

"I really don't know. Now, enough about them. Tell me about your morning. Don't leave out a single detail. What is it like at the Medical Research Council? I really want to know."

Connor told her all about his interview. "For me, the best part was the collaboration among the scientists."

"They were probably putting on their Sunday manners for you," Mary Elizabeth said with a smile. "Remember, you were interviewing them as much as they were interviewing you."

Connor laughed. "If they wanted to hire me to empty the wastebaskets, I think I would've accepted the position. Working for the Medical Research Council is all I ever wanted to do. The research projects that they are working on are really exciting. Of course, I can't go into much detail, but it is groundbreaking research." He then added excitedly, "I can't believe it. This position has regular business hours. And every weekend off. I can have a regular life."

"Regular life? What is that?" Mary Elizabeth asked. "Really, Connor, I'm very happy for you. I know you will make us all proud."

"Have you heard any more about your fellowship?"

"As a matter of fact, I have," Mary Elizabeth said. "Apparently, *fellowship* means precisely that—FELLOWship."

"Huh? Sorry, I'm not following you."

"The hospital is rescinding my fellowship because I am not a fellow. They have finally realized that I am a woman. Apparently, some of the doctors would not feel comfortable working with me. Of course, they are very sorry and hope I can make alternative plans."

Connor reached out his hand to her. "Oh, Mary Elizabeth."

"Well, it's better that I find out how things are now than show up and have them slam the door in my face."

"Although," Connor said with a wicked smile, "I would have liked to see the expression on their faces when they discovered Dr. M. E. Senty's true identity. I would have recorded it all on film."

Mary Elizabeth could not help but smile. "Yes, that would have been grand."

"What are you going to do now?"

"I honestly have no idea. I've already given notice to my landlady, and she has found another boarder. So in a few days, I will be homeless as well as jobless."

"I doubt that will be true. You are too good of a doctor not to find a position."

Mary Elizabeth said, "Thanks, Connor. You know just how to cheer me up." She looked at her watch. "Sorry, I have to leave now." She got up with her tray. "But thank you for having supper with me, and congratulations again on your new job. I am truly happy for you."

Connor also got up with his tray. "Thanks. Here, I'll walk back up with you. I still have to collect my things from the lounge."

When they arrived back on the seventh floor, Connor walked to the lounge, and Mary Elizabeth walked over to the nurses' station. Matron Carruthers was on duty tonight. "May I have Mr. Thornbury's chart, please?"

"What are you doing back here? I thought you left for the day," Matron Carruthers said.

"I still have a few things to do. Mr. Thornbury's chart, please."

"You know, we are perfectly capable of taking care of our patients without you around all the time," Matron Carruthers said as she handed the chart to Mary Elizabeth.

Mary Elizabeth ignored her remark and instead concentrated on Mr. Thornbury's chart. His blood pressure had been taken sixty minutes earlier, and it was on the low side. Mary Elizabeth became very concerned. "Matron Carruthers, please bring a blood pressure cuff to Mr. Thornbury's room. I will meet you there." She walked quickly to his room, and as she walked in, she could tell that his breathing was labored. She took out her stethoscope and examined him. She could hear considerable congestion. He looked as though he were sleeping. His heartbeat was slow and irregular. By this time, Matron Carruthers was at her side. Mary Elizabeth put the cuff on him, and her suspicions were confirmed. His blood pressure was even lower. Mr. Thornbury had lost consciousness. She checked his feet. They were cold, and she could see that his feet and legs were mottled in appearance.

"Call for Dr. Applegate. Mr. Thornbury has taken a turn for the worse. Notify his family and ask them to come in. And if he has any religious preference, alert the hospital chaplain," Mary Elizabeth directed.

Matron Carruthers quickly left the room. Mary Elizabeth held the man's hand. She talked to him and told him that he was not alone. She did not know if, at that point, he could hear her, but she continued to speak to him.

Dr. Applegate came in and took out his stethoscope, listening. He nodded to Mary Elizabeth. The Anglican chaplain came next. He began the prayers for the dying. Matron Carruthers came in and reported that his family was on their way.

Mary Elizabeth said, "Please unhook the IV line from Mr. Thornbury. He does not need it anymore." She then quietly asked Dr. Applegate to join her outside the room.

"I fear that Mr. Thornbury has slipped too far. I can't think of anything to do that would reverse his decline."

"You are correct, Dr. Senty. Sometimes, we just have to let nature take its course."

Mary Elizabeth looked at her watch. The time was 6:10. "I can stay with him for about forty-five minutes before my family conference for Mrs. Plinkton. I hope the family will arrive before then."

"I will make sure that Matron Carruthers knows that either you or I will speak to the family."

"Thank you, Dr. Applegate."

With that, she went back into the room and pulled over a chair. She sat down and picked up Mr. Thornbury's hand. She then softly said to Matron Carruthers that Dr. Applegate would like to speak with her.

The nurse left the room. By this time, the chaplain had finished his prayers. He walked over and picked up Mr. Thornbury's other hand. It was 6:42 p.m. when Matron Carruthers came in and said that the family had arrived. Mary Elizabeth nodded and went out into the hall.

Mrs. Thornbury was accompanied by a young man in his twenties and two younger girls in their late teens. They all wore anxious looks on their faces.

Mary Elizabeth began, "Mr. Thornbury's condition has deteriorated. His lungs are no longer responding to the antibiotics, and he has lost consciousness. I am sorry. Dr. Applegate and I feel that there is nothing more we can do for him. The hospital chaplain is in with him now. While he is no longer able to respond, I do believe he can still hear you. Matron Carruthers will take care of you. Please, do not be afraid to ask for what you need. I am so sorry. Do you have any questions?"

Mrs. Thornbury asked through her tears, "Is he suffering?"

"We are doing everything we can to make him comfortable. At this point, I do not believe he is suffering. He is just sleeping away."

Then Mrs. Thornbury asked, "How . . . how long?"

"We cannot say for sure," Mary Elizabeth responded truthfully. "Now, would you like to go in and see him?"

Mary Elizabeth opened the door, and the family went in. The chaplain went over and introduced himself to them. Mary Elizabeth walked down to the nurses' station. "Matron Carruthers, could you please see that there are enough chairs for Mr. Thornbury's family? And also see to their needs. They will be keeping vigil tonight."

"Yes, Doctor." Matron Carruthers started down the hall.

As an afterthought, Mary Elizabeth said, "And when Mrs. Plinkton's family comes, could you show them into the conference room? Also, Miss Maxwell, the dietitian, will be joining us. It is a very busy night tonight, so ask for help if you need it."

CHAPTER 11

A BUSY EVENING

Mary Elizabeth looked at her watch. The time was now 6:50 p.m.

"Are Mrs. Plinkton's discharge papers ready for her?" Mary Elizabeth asked Nurse Daly, who was now at the nurses' station.

Nurse Daly replied, "Yes, they are in her chart."

"Very good. I will take her chart with me," Mary Elizabeth said as she walked down the hall to the junior doctors' lounge. She sat at the table and went through her notes one more time.

A few minutes before seven, she walked into the conference room. Miss Maxwell, the dietitian, was already in the room. Mary Elizabeth went over to greet her.

Soon Mrs. Plinkton entered, being pushed in a wheelchair by an orderly. She was like a queen with her entourage. Dutifully following her were her husband, son, and daughter. After introductions were made, Mary Elizabeth explained Mrs. Plinkton's condition and all the restrictions that were part of her recovery. She then turned the meeting over to Miss Maxwell. Then, it was time for questions. The conference ended at 7:50 p.m. Mary Elizabeth bade the family goodbye and explained that she would not be here when Mrs. Plinkton came back for her follow-up visit in two weeks. She promised to brief the new doctor about her case. She watched as the happy family left the floor.

Mary Elizabeth once again thanked Miss Maxwell for meeting with the family.

Miss Maxwell said, "No, thank you, Dr. Senty. It was my pleasure. Doing patient education is my favorite part of the job. I wish more doctors would take advantage of our services."

"Your services are much appreciated. You have a good evening now."

"You too, Dr. Senty. Good night," Miss Maxwell said as she walked to the lifts.

Mary Elizabeth went into the lounge and hung up her lab coat in her locker. She folded her raincoat over her arm and picked up her purse. She dropped off Mrs. Plinkton's chart at the nurses' station and then headed for room 712 and knocked on the door.

She heard Harold's voice say, "Come in."

Mary Elizabeth walked in and found Harold sitting in bed, working on a crossword puzzle. As soon as he saw her, he smiled and said, "Come in, Miss Emme, come in."

"Hope I am not keeping you up. My meeting just finished."

"No, not at all. Come sit down. You look like you have had a very busy day."

"Yes, it has been quite a day. Thank you. Did Dr. Applegate stop in before he left this evening?"

"Yes, but our visit was cut short. One of the nurses came in and said that he was needed elsewhere. It sounded serious. I hope everything turned out all right."

"We can add that intention to our Rosary tonight," Mary Elizabeth said. "Did Dr. Applegate tell you anything about your doctor for tomorrow?"

"Just that I would like this doctor. He said that besides being very competent, this doctor has one of the best bedside manners that he has ever seen."

Mary Elizabeth was surprised. "That is very high praise coming from Dr. Applegate."

"He also said that this doctor is a fourth-year junior doctor whose employment plans recently changed. He was going to tell me more, but then the nurse came in, and he left. What can you tell me about this doctor? If you helped choose him for me, you must know him pretty well too."

"You could say that. Did he tell you the doctor's name?"

"No. He said that you would tell me."

"Oh," was all she said. There was a long silence.

"Miss Emme? Are you all right?" The concerned tone of his voice matched the troubled look on his face.

Mary Elizabeth reached for his hand. She had a very serious look on her face that Harold had never seen. "I am finding it very difficult to tell you. I am afraid . . ." Her voice got quieter as it trailed off.

Harold reached over and put his other hand on top of hers. "Emme," he said kindly, "you don't have to be afraid to tell me anything."

Mary Elizabeth took a deep breath and said, "The name of your new doctor is Dr. Senty."

"Dr. Senty," Harold repeated.

"But I am afraid that you won't give this doctor a chance."

"Why wouldn't I give this doctor a chance?"

Tears began forming in Mary Elizabeth's eyes as she said, "I am afraid you will take one look at this doctor and make your mind up, and that will be that. I have seen it happen time and time again. I just couldn't bear it if that happened tomorrow."

"Emme, look at me," Harold said.

Mary Elizabeth looked into his soft brown eyes as a few silent tears fell down her face.

He said, "I give you my word that I will withhold any judgment until Dr. Senty finishes with my physical examination. Then I will give both you and Dr. Applegate my honest assessment. Is that acceptable?"

Mary Elizabeth nodded. She reached into her pocket and found her handkerchief and dried her tears. Then she smiled. "Yes, only because I know you are a man of your word."

Harold laughed. "Now, let's have no more talk of doctors tonight. I can see that you have had a very long day. Shall we say our Rosary?"

"Is it the Sorrowful Mysteries tonight?" Mary Elizabeth asked.

"Yes, I believe it is."

"Would you mind leading again?"

"No, not at all." And so they began their prayer. Mary Elizabeth silently dedicated her Rosary to Mr. Thornbury and his family. As their prayer continued, Mary Elizabeth began to feel a sense of peace enter her troubled heart. By the time the Rosary was completed, Mary Elizabeth felt much better.

She asked, "Would you like me to give you a back rub tonight?"

"I would love that. But are you sure you just don't want to go home? You look tired."

"I also keep my word. This afternoon, I promised that if you would stay, I would give you one, but only if you wanted one. Here, I will step out of the room for a few minutes and let you prepare for the night. I will be back shortly." Mary Elizabeth walked down to the nurses' station. Matron Carruthers was at the desk.

When she saw Mary Elizabeth she said, "Dr. Senty! What are you still doing here? You should go home. You look terrible."

"I will be leaving shortly. How is the Thornbury family?"

"Mr. Thornbury passed away about seven thirty. Dr. McCafferty was on the floor, and he certified the death. The family has gone home, and the funeral directors have already picked up the body."

Mary Elizabeth said, "Thank you for all of your help this evening with Mr. Thornbury and his family and Mrs. Plinkton and her family. May I have Mr. Baxter's chart? How is he doing? How is his postoperative pain?"

"He hasn't complained of any pain."

Mary Elizabeth looked at his chart. "His pain medication was given at five. His last vitals were taken at 5:10. Has anyone checked in on him since then?"

"It has been a very busy night," Matron Carruthers said defensively. "We do the best we can."

Mary Elizabeth said sternly, "Bring a thermometer and a blood pressure cuff to his room." She turned and walked quickly down the hall. Knocking softly on his door, she walked into his room. Mr. Baxter was wide awake.

"Good evening, Mr. Baxter. How are you doing this evening?"

When he saw her, he said, "My leg hurts. Did you fix it?"

"Yes, the orthopedic surgeon said it was a success. We had to put some screws in place, so you have some hardware now in your leg, but the bone should heal fine. Would you mind if I examined you?"

"No, not at all."

Mary Elizabeth took her stethoscope and listened to his heart and lungs. By this time, Matron Carruthers had arrived with the thermometer and the blood pressure cuff.

"Thank you. You may go now," Mary Elizabeth said curtly.

She continued with her examination and charted the results herself. When she was finished, she said, "You seem to be doing well after your surgery, although I do hear some congestion in your lungs. Does it hurt when you take a deep breath?"

"Yes, it does," he answered.

"That is to be expected after a long surgery like you had today. So, what we do for now is to watch it."

Mr. Baxter began to cough.

"That's it. If you have to cough, cough. It helps dislodge the fluid. Very good."

"Coughing makes my lungs and my leg hurt worse."

"Yes, it will. I am going to prescribe a stronger pain medication for you. The nurse will inject it into your IV, and that should make you comfortable. Now, I want you to be honest about your pain. Admitting you feel pain is not a sign of weakness, or unmanly, or anything like that. I don't want you suffering in silence, because pain actually delays the healing process. Your recovery process is going to be long enough as it is, so we don't want any delays, do we?"

"No, we sure don't."

"Good. The pain medication might also make you sleepy. Don't fight it. Sleep. When you sleep, your body can spend more time repairing itself. You and I are partners in your healing. We have to work together for you to get back on your feet, both of them." Mary Elizabeth stuck out her hand. "Partners?"

Mr. Baxter shook her hand and answered firmly, "Partners."

"Good. Now, do you have any questions for me?"

"Just one," Mr. Baxter said with a sheepish grin. "When do you sleep? I saw you early this morning, and you are still here."

Mary Elizabeth laughed. "I can see you are a sharp one. That is a fair question. Today was an extraordinarily busy day. Thankfully, they are not always this busy. I will be going home shortly. I will see you tomorrow morning. Good night."

After she left his room, she went down to the nurses' station and made some notes in Mr. Baxter's chart. She handed the chart back to Matron Carruthers. In a stern voice, she said, "See that Mr. Baxter receives his pain medication at once. I also want his vitals taken every four hours. If there are any unusual spikes, contact the doctor on duty. Do you have any questions for me?"

"No, Doctor."

"Good night." Mary Elizabeth turned and walked back to room 712. Harold was already in bed. When he saw her, he said, "I thought you forgot about me and went home. But then I saw you left your purse."

"Sorry. I guess I was away longer than I'd intended. Something came up that needed my attention."

"You must have a pretty important job with all your responsibilities and the hours you keep. What exactly do you do around here?"

"Please, can I tell you tomorrow? It is getting late."

"Yes, yes, of course. You can tell me tomorrow." Harold flipped over onto his stomach.

After Mary Elizabeth washed up, she squirted the lotion on her hands. She began a steady movement up and down his back. Moving her hands over his shoulder muscles, she reported, "Good. Your body is telling me I don't have to work so hard tonight. Your shoulder muscles feel much more relaxed than last night."

"All the credit goes to you, Emme," Harold replied. "You are good for me."

Mary Elizabeth continued to work in silence. After fifteen minutes, she stopped. She could tell that Harold was quite relaxed. In fact, he was almost asleep. She whispered, "Good night, Harold. I will see you tomorrow morning."

There was no reply. Mary Elizabeth tucked his blankets around him, shut off his overhead light and left quietly.

As she walked home, she thought about her grandfather's words that Dr. Applegate had recited to her. That brought her a little peace, although her heart ached as she thought about him and the rest of her family. She missed them so much. She wearily climbed the stairs into her rented room. Placing her purse down on her desk, she got ready for bed. Before she got into bed, she opened her purse and took out a plane ticket. She looked at it once again. It was a one-way ticket from London to Boston for Sunday, August 30, 1959. That night in bed she tried to figure out what to do next. She prayed, *Oh God! What am I going to do? Sunday is only five days away. I only have five days to come up with a new plan for my future. Please, help me!* The exhaustion of the day caught up with her. She fell asleep repeating, *Thy will be done. Thy will be done.*

Wednesday, August 26

CHAPTER 12

A NEW DAY

Just as Dr. Applegate had predicted, the next morning was clear and sunny. It was going to be another hot day. Even though it was shortly after six o'clock, Mary Elizabeth could already feel the humidity as she walked the four streets to the hospital from her boardinghouse. As if she needed encouragement for what lay ahead, the cardinals and the robins voiced their support in song. Their messages of merriment and hopefulness were impossible to miss.

Yes, today was definitely a day of reckoning for her. No more avoiding it. Today, she would finally be completely honest with Mr. Merton. She had only met him two days earlier, and yet he had become very important to her. In his presence, it was almost like being home among her family. She always looked forward to their visits. As she walked along, it finally hit her. Because he had not been her patient, she could just be herself around him. And the best part was that he really never expected anything from her. They were just two small-town people who had found each other in the big city and enjoyed each other's company.

And today, all of that was going to change. Today, she was Dr. Senty, and he would be her patient, Mr. Merton. As she reached the hospital and passed through the revolving doors, she prayed for the courage to accept whatever might happen. How this day would unfold was anyone's guess.

As Mary Elizabeth entered the junior doctors' lounge, as usual, there was Dr. Batra working on his charts.

"Morning, Ruhan," she called out.

"Good morning, Mary Elizabeth," he answered. He looked at his watch. "You're here a bit early this morning. How was your evening?"

"Long, and very busy." She paused. "Mr. Thornbury died last evening."

"Om Shanti," Ruhan said.

"Thank you, Ruhan. And I fear that this morning is going to pick up where last night left off." She went to her locker and put on her lab coat. "See you later."

Mary Elizabeth went to the nurses' station. Matron Stewart was at the desk. "Matron Stewart, could I please have Mr. Baxter's chart?"

Matron Stewart retrieved it for her, and Mary Elizabeth spent a few minutes studying its contents at the desk. "May I have a thermometer and the blood pressure cuff, please?"

"Do you want me to send a nurse with you? She can take those readings for you," Matron Stewart said.

"No, thank you. Your nurses have plenty to do. I don't mind. I will be examining him anyway," Mary Elizabeth said.

"Am I seeing that Yankee self-reliance we Brits always hear so much about?" Matron Stewart asked with a chuckle.

"Mmm. Never thought about it," Mary Elizabeth answered back thoughtfully. Then, with a firm nod, she said, "Yes, yes, I guess that's it." She left Matron Stewart with a smile and walked down the hall.

She knocked gently on Mr. Baxter's door and walked in. He was still sleeping soundly. This was one of the parts of her job that Mary Elizabeth disliked. It seemed cruel to wake patients from sleep, especially when rest and sleep were what they needed. She gently touched his arm.

"Mr. Baxter," she called. Again a little louder, she called, "Mr. Baxter. It's Dr. Senty."

"Huh? Oh, sorry. Is it morning already? Wow! I had the weirdest dream." Ronald Baxter was trying to wake up.

"So sorry to wake you. Just want to take your temperature and your blood pressure," Mary Elizabeth said.

"How come you are doing that? Isn't that a nurse's job?"

"Really now, you too? What is this today?"

"Just curious."

"Well, Matron Stewart thinks it has to do with my being an American. So, there you go. Now, you just think about that while I stick this thermometer under your tongue. Ready?"

Mr. Baxter readily complied. Mary Elizabeth then took his blood pressure. She removed the thermometer from his mouth and charted the results. Then she listened to his heart and lungs.

She reported, "Your lungs still sound a bit congested. I am going to schedule you for a chest X-ray today just to get a better look at what is going on in there."

"Yes, Doctor."

"Now, how is your pain this morning?"

"My pain is definitely still there, but much better than it was last night. And it still hurts when I breathe."

"Is the pain tolerable at this level?

"Yes, it is."

"Good, because this medicine is strong and can be addicting if not used correctly. So the trick is to use the least amount possible to get the desired results."

"I understand. No, this is a tolerable level."

"Good. Before I go, do you have any questions for me?"

"Will you be in to see me later on today?"

"Yes, I will be in to see you later on today with the results of your chest X-ray," Mary Elizabeth said.

Mr. Baxter said, "All right. Thank you."

"You have a good day, and I will see you later." She smiled.

Mary Elizabeth walked back to the nurses' station. The nursing shift was changing. Matron Stewart and Matron Hartly were busy going through the patient files. Mary Elizabeth wrote her orders. She then waited patiently until they were finished.

"That's it for me," Matron Stewart said. "See you tomorrow." She left the floor.

"Yes, Doctor?" Matron Hartly asked the lingering Dr. Senty.

"Please schedule a chest X-ray for Mr. Baxter. Give him an extra bump in his pain medication, thirty minutes prior to them taking him down. Moving him at this point is going to be extremely painful for him, so I would like to minimize the pain as much as possible. I also think it would be beneficial for Mr. Baxter to be around people his own age, so if you can swing it, maybe have the younger nurses attend him?"

The nurse began to laugh. "Do I detect a little matchmaking going on?"

Mary Elizabeth laughed. "It couldn't hurt." She walked down to the junior doctors' lounge. She removed her coat and laid it over a chair.

She walked down the hall to room 712. She knocked and walked inside. Harold was sitting in his bed saying his morning prayers. He looked up. When he saw her, he smiled and said, "Good morning, Miss Emme. What brings you here so early?"

"Good morning, Harold," Mary Elizabeth said as she sat down in the chair next to his bed. "How did you sleep last night?"

"Very well, thank you." He put down his prayer book and looked at her expectantly.

There was an awkward silence as Mary Elizabeth couldn't quite figure out what to say next. Finally, she said, "Harold, there is something I want to tell you. But first, I need you to know that I never intended to deceive you. Do you remember when you asked me my name that day in the park, and I said it was Emme?"

"Yes." Harold looked confused. "Isn't your name Emme?"

"Well, yes, it is. But 'Emme' is my nickname. Only my family and my friends back home in Minnesota call me that. No one except you and now Dr. Applegate here in England knows me by that name."

"Oh," Harold said. "And you would rather that I not call you by that name anymore?"

"This is getting so complicated," Mary Elizabeth said. "I liked it when you called me Emme. I still do. You see, I haven't had anyone call me by that name in five years. And I guess, that day in the park, I was feeling a bit homesick. I just wanted to hear someone call me by that familiar name once again. But when I come in later this morning with Dr. Applegate, he will not be calling me Emme. He will be calling me by my full name. But when we are alone together, if you still want to call me Emme, please do."

"So, you would rather I don't call you Emme in front of Dr. Applegate and my new doctor?"

"Yes, that's right." Mary Elizabeth sounded relieved. "When you say it like that, it doesn't sound that complicated at all. Thank you, Harold." She smiled at him and looked at her watch. She patted his hand and got up. "It is time for me to go down to Dr. Applegate's office. I shall see you in a bit."

"But, Emme, what do you want me to call you?" Harold called after her.

"Just follow Dr. Applegate's lead," Mary Elizabeth said as she walked out the door. Her first stop was the junior doctors' lounge, where she donned her white lab coat. Then she walked to the nurses' station.

"Matron Hartly, may I have Mr. Merton's chart, please?" Mary Elizabeth asked. "And a new intake sheet. I will be giving Mr. Merton a physical examination later this morning, so if you could have the necessary instruments out on a tray and ready to go, I would appreciate it. It will be a full physical, so I will require a scale. Thank you."

"Yes, Doctor. Wasn't some of that already done?" Matron Hartly inquired.

"This morning, we are starting from scratch with Mr. Merton. But Dr. Applegate's orders still stand. I will be doing all the procedures. Oh yes, hold his breakfast until after his physical is complete, please."

"Yes, Doctor." Matron Hartly sighed. "Silly question, I know, but do you want a nurse to accompany you?"

"We shall see. I will come to the desk after the intake and then decide."

Mary Elizabeth turned and walked down to Dr. Applegate's office. She walked in and knocked on his open door.

"Come in, Dr. Senty," Dr. Applegate called. He was seated behind his desk. When he saw her, he got up and said, "Are you ready to meet your new patient?"

"Dr. Senty is more than ready to meet Mr. Merton. But I do have to say, Miss Emme is going to miss her friend Harold," Mary Elizabeth said.

"I cannot pretend to speak for Mr. Merton, but I do think that there is a very good chance that Miss Emme will see Harold again. I have it on good authority that they will be going out to lunch later today."

"I hope you are right, Dr. Applegate."

CHAPTER 13

Exams for Harold and Emme

They left his office and walked down the hall. When they got to the door of room 712, Dr. Applegate said, "Here, you wait outside. I would like to speak to Mr. Merton alone. I will come back out to get you in a minute." Dr. Applegate knocked on the door.

Mary Elizabeth could hear him say, "Good morning, Harold," as he walked through the door. But then the door closed, and she could not hear anything else. She clutched Harold's chart tighter as butterflies started dancing inside her.

Inside the room, Harold said, "Good morning, Basil. Where is Miss Emme? I thought she would be here."

"Miss Emme will be along a little later. Although, she did tell me that she is still looking forward to going to lunch with you. Not to change the subject, but when you called last month looking for a junior doctor to mentor, I immediately thought of this young doctor. Over the past four years, I have seen Dr. Senty develop into a confident and competent doctor. It must be all those prayers you say, because Dr. Senty was set to take a position in the United States, but within the last twenty-four hours, those plans have changed, and Dr. Senty is now available. To be sure, you will have to make up your own mind, but I am telling you right now that you would be a damn fool if you did not offer Dr. Senty the position in Bellechester."

"That is high praise, indeed, coming from you, Basil. I can't wait to meet this Dr. Senty."

"Good. Dr. Senty is standing right outside." Dr. Applegate opened the door and called, "Dr. Senty, you may come in now."

Mary Elizabeth took a deep breath and, still clutching the chart, walked confidently in the door. She went up to Harold, held out her hand, and said, "Good morning, Mr. Merton. I am Dr. Mary Elizabeth Senty. Pleased to make your acquaintance." She smiled her familiar smile.

Harold took her hand. "Basil? Emme? What is going on here? Are you playing a joke on me?" Harold inquired with a hint of anger in his voice.

"No, Mr. Merton, I would never do that," Mary Elizabeth said. "That day in the park, I just never revealed to you my entire name."

Dr. Applegate added, "Dr. Senty is one of my fourth-year junior doctors. Yesterday morning, she came to me and asked if she could be your doctor, but I had already assigned Dr. Westby to your case."

Harold finally released Mary Elizabeth's hand.

"I would still like to be your doctor, Mr. Merton. But only if you want me to be. It is totally up to you." She stood next to his bed, hugging his chart.

After she finished speaking, Harold studied her face carefully. He noticed that she wore a stoic expression, although her chin jutted out just a bit. She no longer looked at him directly, but rather, her eyes were focused beyond him to a spot on the wall. She was clutching his chart so tightly that her knuckles turned white. In his mind, he replayed the conversation they'd had last night. He recalled how afraid she was that he would not give his new doctor a chance. He also remembered that he assured her that he would be fair. Yes, he had given his word. He could not and would not disappoint her.

Harold finally spoke. "Basil, I would be pleased to have Dr. Senty attend me." He watched as Mary Elizabeth's entire body relaxed. A smile returned to her face. "However, Dr. Senty, I give you fair warning," he said sternly. "I have been known to be a difficult patient."

Mary Elizabeth finally looked at him with her dancing blue eyes. "Yes, I have heard that about you, Mr. Merton," she replied. "But that's okay, I enjoy a challenge."

Dr. Applegate let out an audible sigh of relief. "I can see I am no longer needed here. I will let Dr. Senty get on with the exam. Harold, I will be in later this morning with Dr. Senty after our morning conference to hear your report." He walked out of the room, leaving them alone.

"May I sit down, Mr. Merton?" Mary Elizabeth asked politely.

"Of course. But, please call me Harold."

"As you wish." Mary Elizabeth said.

What happens first?" Harold asked.

"I know that some of what we are going to do this morning you have already done with Dr. Westby, but I would like to redo the intake evaluation for my own benefit. Would that be acceptable to you?"

"Yes, that makes perfect sense to me."

"So, what brought you all the way to Mother of Mercy Hospital from Bellechester?"

Harold knew that this was not the time to tell her the real reason for his visit. But what he did end up telling her was the truth. He described how he had been feeling the past few months.

"Since you have been here, do you have any additional symptoms or anything else we should check out?"

"No, but sometimes it seems as if my mind is working slower than usual, and I do find myself drinking a lot of water."

Mary Elizabeth listened attentively and made notes. "When was the last time you saw a doctor?"

"Last February, I had pneumonia. I was in the hospital for almost two weeks."

"When was the last time you had a physical?"

"Oh my, it has been so long, I don't even remember," Harold answered.

"Do you know who holds your medical records?"

"Dr. Upton in Glendale would have them. Glendale is about six miles west of Bellechester. It is the largest town in the area and is where the local hospital is located."

"Are you presently taking any medications?"

"No."

"How are you sleeping?"

"Sometimes, I wake up at night and I start thinking about my worries, and then it is hard to fall back to sleep." Harold found it easy to talk with her. Because they had spent some time together, he did not feel his usual awkwardness or shyness. Even though the doctor sitting next to him was wearing a white coat and taking notes, she was still Emme.

"May I ask," Mary Elizabeth inquired, "what are some of the things you worry about?"

"Mostly, I worry about the future."

Mary Elizabeth smiled. "To be honest, worrying about the future has kept me awake lately too."

Harold smiled back at her. "Somehow, I find that very comforting."

Mary Elizabeth put down her pen and said, "Thank you for answering all my questions. Now, do you remember what I told you the other day about not being afraid to ask questions?"

"Yes."

"Well, I meant it. So if you have any questions about what I am doing or why I am doing something, please ask."

"I will."

"Now, you just sit back and rest for a few minutes. I need to get some supplies for the next few exams. I'll be right back."

Mary Elizabeth left and went to the nurses' station. "Matron Hartly, can you please get a Dr. Upton in Glendale on the phone for me? I would like to speak with him regarding Mr. Merton."

"Yes, Doctor."

"And I will take my supplies now, if they are ready. And yes, if you could have a nurse roll down the scale for me and assist, I would appreciate that."

Matron Hartly teased her. "Wait! Let me mark down the date and time. I do believe it has been a while since I have heard those words come from your mouth." Then, more seriously, she continued, "All the nurses are with patients right now, but as soon as I can, I will send someone down with the scale."

Mary Elizabeth checked the supplies on her tray. Mentally, she went through the physical in her head and double-checked to see that she had the correct instruments. "Here is the Vacutainer® needle but no tubes," she said.

"What colors do you want?" Matron Hartly asked.

"Give me a purple, gold, and light blue, please."

"Certainly, Doctor." Matron Hartly left and retrieved them from the supply closet. When she returned, she asked, "Is there anything else you need, Doctor?"

"No, this is good for now. Thank you." With her tray in hand, she returned to Mr. Merton's room.

When Harold saw Mary Elizabeth with her tray, he said, "My goodness, what is all this?"

"How about I explain as we go along? Do you think you can give me that urine sample now?"

"Yes."

"Good. Here is your container." She handed it to him as he headed toward the bathroom.

A few minutes later, he returned to the room and handed her the sample. She put it on the tray and asked Harold if he would sit on the side of the bed. Then she went and washed her hands. She took the thermometer off the tray and asked

Harold to put it under his tongue. She then asked for his wrist and said she would take his pulse.

"Temperature is ninety-eight point four. Pulse is seventy-three. Both are good readings." She wrote the numbers in his chart. "Now, I would like to take your blood pressure. May I?"

Harold asked, "Are you sure you know how to do it?"

Mary Elizabeth smiled as she fitted the cuff on him. "Pretty sure. I have never gotten any complaints yet."

"There is always a first time."

"Well, why don't you watch me? When I am done, you can tell me how I did. Is that fair?"

"Yes, that is fair."

"Now the cuff is going to squeeze your arm for a minute, so bear with me." Mary Elizabeth began to pump the bulb.

As the cuff tightened on his arm, Harold inhaled.

"Eighty-eight over fifty-six," Mary Elizabeth announced. She removed the cuff from his arm and recorded the numbers in his chart.

"Those readings are a bit low. Are you sure you did it correctly?"

"Yes, I am sure. Actually, those numbers do not surprise me."

Harold was still sitting on the side of the bed, and Mary Elizabeth had just tested his reflexes when Harold asked, "Emme, why did you become a doctor? It is not a typical career choice for a woman."

Mary Elizabeth stopped what she was doing and looked at Harold. A slight smile crept over her face, and she said, "I wondered when that question would come up."

"If that question is too personal, you don't have to answer it."

"No, that's okay." She laughed. "Believe me, you are not the first person to ask me that question. My stock answer is: 'I became a doctor because I wanted to help people when they were at their most vulnerable and when they needed help the most. I was given the opportunity to go to school and the encouragement to follow my dream.' That usually satisfies the questioner."

"Does it really?" Harold asked in a surprised voice.

Mary Elizabeth looked at him. She smiled and said, "I should've known that my routine answer wouldn't be good enough for you, Harold. Do you really want to know?"

Harold said seriously, "Yes, Emme, I do."

Seeing how earnest he was, Mary Elizabeth put down the reflex hammer on the tray and sat down in the chair next to his bed. "I usually don't share this with my patients, but since you and I were friends before we had a doctor-patient relationship, I will tell you the entire story. This might take a few minutes." She looked at him and said, "Just remember, you asked."

Harold nodded.

Mary Elizabeth began her story. "Growing up, I always knew that I was different from most girls. I found I was happiest when working alongside my father and grandfather out in the barn or in the fields. As I grew older, I decided I wanted a career instead of getting married and raising a family like most of the girls I knew. When I was in grade school, I used to enjoy reading biographies of famous people. I believe I was eleven years old when I read the story of Elizabeth Blackwell, who was the first woman in America to become a doctor. Her story made a big impression on me. I really admired her. And then, a few months later, I was home with my grandmother, and we were watching my younger siblings. My mother had taken my older sister into town for her music lesson. My dad and grandfather were out in the fields . . ." Mary Elizabeth paused. "Let's see. At that time, I had five younger siblings we were watching. All of a sudden, my grandmother grabbed her chest and collapsed on the floor. She stopped breathing. I didn't know how to help her. All I could think to do was get on the telephone and tell the operator what happened and ask her to call for the doctor. Then I just left her and ran out to the fields as fast as I could to get my dad and grandfather. By the time we all got back to the house, the doctor had already arrived. He tried to revive her, but it was too late. My grandma was gone."

Tears filled Mary Elizabeth's eyes. "I didn't know what to do. I didn't know how to help her.

I felt so helpless. That bothered me for a long time." She paused. "It still does. Everyone said I did the right thing in trying to get help, but I blamed myself. I decided that when I got older, I would learn what to do in a situation like that. So that further solidified my determination to become a doctor.

"Luckily, when I got to high school, I discovered I was good at science classes. With lots of help, I attended our local all-women's college where I took more science classes. The nuns taught us to dream big. We were never to be satisfied with 'what is' but to strive for 'what could be.' They made us feel that we could accomplish anything we set our minds and wills to do. They knew what they were talking about, because many of my teachers were the first women in their order to get advanced degrees in their fields of study. They were wonderful role models. Real trailblazers.

"In my junior year, I finally confided to my advisor about my admiration for Elizabeth Blackwell and my desire to become a doctor. In my senior year, she arranged for me to take premed classes at the Benedictine men's college down the road. I found the studies challenging, and I also discovered that my grades were as good as the men's, so I got up the courage to apply to medical school. I was accepted, and so ten years later, here I am." Mary Elizabeth got up from the chair and rolled the portable table over that held her instruments.

Harold was silent for a long time before he said quietly, "Thank you. I feel privileged that you shared your story with me."

Mary Elizabeth said with a smile, "Well, remember, you did ask."

Harold smiled. "Yes, I did." Then, in his normal voice, he asked, "Now, what's next?"

"Let's do the blood-draw," Mary Elizabeth said.

"That is where the trouble started with Dr. Westby yesterday," Harold reminded her.

"Harold, you have done splendidly all morning. Look at all we have accomplished. You don't have any complaints against me so far, do you?"

Harold smiled. "You will have to wait and see. Remember, I am waiting until the end to make my report to you and Basil."

Mary Elizabeth smiled and, in her usual upbeat manner, replied, "Fair enough. Do you have a preference which arm I use for the blood-draw?"

Harold stretched out both arms. His right arm was still bruised from Dr. Westby's futile attempts the day before.

"Looks like the left will have to do." She then went to the bathroom and looked around. Not finding what she wanted, she again disappeared out the door and returned a few minutes later with a clean washcloth and large towel. She then soaked the washcloth under hot water for a minute and returned to his side.

"What's all that for?" Harold inquired.

"Can you hold your arm straight for me and make a fist?"

Harold did as she asked. With her finger, she tapped the veins in the crook of his arm.

"I suspect that you are still dehydrated from your travels on Monday. Your veins are hiding. So we will just have to coax them out by putting a warm compress on your arm for a few minutes." Mary Elizabeth felt the washcloth and then placed it on his arm. "There, that is not too hot for you, is it?"

"No, it is fine."

"Good." She then wrapped the towel around the washcloth. "We will just let the warmth do its work."

As she was speaking, there was a knock on the door. Matron Hartly came in with the scale. "Dr. Senty, you have a phone call at the nurses' station."

"Thank you, Matron Hartly. Excuse me, Harold, I shall return. I need to take this call."

CHAPTER 14

$\mathcal{T}$HE TRUTH ABOUT HAROLD

Mary Elizabeth hurried to the desk and picked up the phone.

"Dr. Senty speaking."

"Dr. Senty, Dr. Upton. What can I do for you?"

"A patient of yours, Harold Merton, has come to Mother of Mercy Hospital here in London for a physical examination. He says that you hold his medical records."

"Yes. The last time I saw Harold Merton was last winter, when his priest friend from Bellechester brought him in with a severe case of bacterial pneumonia. Stubborn old fool. He almost waited too long. Luckily, he responded well to the antibiotics, but it was touch and go for a while. He was in the hospital for over two weeks. His blood pressure was a bit high back then."

"Can you tell me the date of his last physical?"

"His chart says 1950. That was before I came here."

"Are his immunizations up to date?"

"Yes, he is very good about that. He will come in for those. The only reason being, he can't administer them himself. Everything is current."

"Anything else from his record that I should know about?"

"Not from the records I have on him. I usually see him only for his vaccinations or when he is really ill. Dr. Merton also keeps a set of his medical records with him at his clinic in Bellechester."

"*Dr.* Merton?"

Dr. Upton laughed. "Did he forget to mention the fact that he is a doctor?"

"Yes, I am afraid he did. What type of medicine does he practice?"

"Why, he is the GP for Bellechester."

"Thank you, Dr. Upton. The information you shared is quite helpful."

"Listen, Dr. Senty. My advice to you is that if Dr. Merton has come in for a physical, then examine him from head to toe because there must be something amiss."

"Be assured, I will be very thorough. Thank you again, Dr. Upton. Goodbye." As Mary Elizabeth hung up the phone, she murmured, "Oh, Harold." She hurried back to his room. When she walked in, she heard Matron Hartly saying, "And you will not find a more conscientious and compassionate one."

When Matron Hartly saw Dr. Senty, she said, "Do you need me for anything?"

"Yes, if you could stay for a few minutes. I was just about to do the blood-draw."

Mary Elizabeth removed the towel from Harold's arm. "See, Mr. Merton, how nicely your veins have popped up for me?" She put on her gloves and applied a tourniquet to Harold's upper arm. She swabbed his arm with an alcohol-soaked cotton ball. Feeling for the vein, she said, "Harold, here comes the poke." She then inserted the needle and drew out the vials of blood. In a minute, she had his arm bandaged, and his blood-draw was all done.

She looked up and asked, "How did I do? That wasn't too uncomfortable for you, was it?"

Harold said, "No, not too bad."

Matron Hartly said, "I told you she is one of our best."

Mary Elizabeth said to Harold, "Let's take your measurements, and then Matron Hartly can take the scale away. Do you think you can stand?"

"Of course," Harold said. Mary Elizabeth helped him up and walked him over to the scale.

"Do you want me to chart?" Matron Hartly asked.

"Yes, that would be great. Thank you." Mary Elizabeth replied.

Harold stepped on the scale. "Five foot eight and one hundred eighty-five pounds," Mary Elizabeth called out.

"Got it," Matron Hartly said as she wrote the numbers in Mr. Merton's chart.

"Thank you for bringing in the scale."

"My pleasure, Dr. Senty," Matron Hartly said as she wheeled out the scale into the hallway.

"Excuse me, Mr. Merton, I shall be right back. Please stay up, walk around the room until I return." Mary Elizabeth grabbed the urine sample and the blood vials and followed the nurse out into the hall.

"Matron Hartly?"

"Yes?"

"I'll walk down with you. Could you put a rush on these, please, and ask the lab to have the results back by eleven?"

"Yes, Doctor."

"Thank you." She placed the blood vials and the urine container on the counter of the nurses' station and then returned to Harold's room.

When Harold saw her, he asked hopefully, "Well, are we about done with my physical?"

"We are almost finished. Only a few more exams to go."

Harold watched as Mary Elizabeth washed her hands and donned a pair of gloves. "And what exams might those be?"

"I will be checking you for any signs of a hernia, and then I will check your prostate. For a gentleman of your age, those exams are a routine part of any physical."

Harold sighed. He knew she was right. He followed her instructions and put himself into her care. She asked him all the right questions, and once again, he was struck by her efficient and competent manner. In a few moments, the unpleasant exams were over.

Mary Elizabeth removed her gloves and washed her hands again. When she came back, she wrote her notes in his chart. "Everything checked out. Although your prostate feels slightly larger than normal, that is not uncommon for a mature gentleman. It feels smooth, and I could detect no irregularities. I also could not detect any hernias. Here, if you can sit on the side of the bed, I will listen to your heart and lungs. Can you take some deep breaths for me?" After that, she asked him to lie down, and she listened to his intestines.

She asked him questions about his digestion, and once again, Harold answered truthfully. She listened carefully and then wrote notes in his chart. Finally, she asked, "Is there anything else you think we should examine?"

"No, I think we have covered everything."

"Do you have any further questions for me?"

"No, I don't believe so."

"When I spoke to Dr. Upton earlier, he said that you were up to date on your immunizations, so as far as I am concerned, your physical is completed."

"You spoke to Dr. Upton?" Harold asked.

"Yes, he was very informative." Mary Elizabeth smiled. "He said that you also keep a copy of your medical records with you in Bellechester. So when I write up my notes from this morning, do you want me to make two copies, one for Dr. Upton and one for you?"

"Yes, if it isn't too much trouble."

"No trouble at all. Have you decided where we are going for lunch?"

"How can I think about lunch when I haven't had my breakfast yet?"

"True enough. I will tell the nurses to bring you your breakfast. When your test results come back from the lab, we can go through them to-gether. Then I will give you my final diagnosis. How does that sound?"

"Thank you, Emme, I mean, Dr. Senty."

"Now I will leave you in peace. Enjoy your breakfast, and I will see you later." When Mary Elizabeth left Harold's room, she went down to the nurses' station.

"Matron Hartly, Mr. Merton is now cleared to receive his breakfast. Did X-Ray say when they could take Mr. Baxter?"

"He is scheduled for ten o'clock. Before you say it, we know to increase his pain medication at nine thirty, and I have one of our younger nurses attending him."

Mary Elizabeth looked at her watch. It was time to get ready for the morning conference. "May I have Mr. Baxter's and Miss Atkinson's charts, please? I still have Mr. Merton's."

Matron Hartly handed her Mr. Baxter's chart. "Dr. Senty, don't you remember?"

"Remember what?"

"Since Friday will be your last day, Miss At-kinson has been moved down to the surgical floor. You released her to Dr. Fleming yesterday. He will be doing her surgery tomorrow to remove her brain tumor. Her primary care will be given to the junior doctor doing his surgery rotation. I knew your long hours were going to catch up with you sooner or later."

"Oh my. How could I have forgotten?"

The kind nurse came over to her and said, "You know, you are allowed to be human once in a while, Dr. Senty. These past few days have been quite intense for you. We have all been looking out for you."

"Really? Have I been that forgetful that I need keepers? Have I forgotten anything else?"

"Just how to take care of yourself. Now get out of here before you are late for your conference."

Mary Elizabeth smiled. "Yes, Matron Hartly, and thank you." She walked down the hall and went into the lounge to get her teacup.

CHAPTER 15

The Final Report

The morning conference did not last as long as usual. Since the fourth-years were leaving at the end of the week, their patient load was dwindling. As their patients were discharged, Dr. Applegate did not assign any more patients to them. The third-year junior doctors were now bearing the load. As they were finishing, Dr. Applegate said, "Dr. Harrington has an announcement to make."

Stuey rose in his place. "My parents are pleased to host a cocktail party for us on Saturday evening at seven o'clock. The dress code is casual. Ruhan and Mary Elizabeth will be staying the weekend, as they will have to clear out of their rented rooms on Friday. It will be our last time together, so I hope you all can make it."

Dr. Applegate said, "Thank you to Dr. Harrington and to his parents. It will be a fitting way to celebrate the end of this cohort. Mrs. Applegate and I will be looking forward to it. Now, the last thing I have to say is that, tomorrow, the third-year junior doctors will be joining us. I will be announcing the pairings, as they will shadow you tomorrow. On Friday, they will be taking over the care of your remaining patients, and you will be with them in an advisory capacity only. Along with the incoming cohort of junior doctors, you will also be the guests of honor at the annual Welcome Luncheon on Friday at noon. After that, you are free to leave. Remember to clear out your lockers. Any questions? Anyone? Hearing none, I will let you get back to work."

As Mary Elizabeth got up to leave, Ruhan said, "We are going to the India Palace tonight after work to celebrate Connor's job. Can you join us? At about six?"

"That sounds wonderful. Now that I am down to two patients, I think I can make it."

"Great."

Mary Elizabeth walked down to the nurses' station. "Matron Hartly, have Mr. Merton's lab reports come back yet?"

"Yes, here they are. And Mr. Baxter is back in his room. Would you like to have his X-rays too?"

"Yes, please." With materials in hand, Mary Elizabeth walked back to the conference room, which had a light box so she could view Mr. Baxter's X-rays. As she put them up, she could see that there was a large amount of fluid forming around both lungs. She made her notes and placed these in his file along with the X-rays.

She then turned her attention to Mr. Merton's labs. His urine and blood tests both showed indicators confirming her suspicion that Harold was indeed dehydrated. She wrote down her diagnosis and treatment plan for his record. She got up and walked back to the nurses' station.

"Matron Hartly, can you set up an IV with a nine percent saline solution for Mr. Merton? Just leave the pole outside his room. You can put the tray with the IV materials in his room. Dr. Applegate and I will be there in a few minutes."

Mary Elizabeth walked down to Dr. Applegate's office. As she walked in, Mrs. Stanfield greeted her. "Dr. Senty, what can I do for you today?"

"I am here to pick up Dr. Applegate. We are going to see Mr. Merton."

She glanced at the phone. "It looks like he is on a call. Would you like to wait, or should I send him down when he is off the phone?"

"I'll go down to Mr. Merton's room, and he can join us when he is free. Thank you, Mrs. Stanfield."

Mary Elizabeth walked back to Mr. Merton's room, knocked, and walked in. "How was your breakfast, Harold?"

"Let's just say that I am looking forward to lunch. Will Basil be joining us?"

"Yes, he should be along shortly. Are you looking forward to going back to Bellechester?"

"Yes, I am. But it has been good to see my old friend Basil again, and I am eagerly anticipating dinner tonight with his wife, Caroline."

"Now, how is it that you know Dr. Applegate and his wife?"

Just as Harold was ready to answer, there was a knock on the door, and a young nurse brought in a tray and put it on the table. "Here are your supplies, Dr. Senty, and the IV is outside."

"Thank you, Nurse."

Harold asked, "What's all this? An IV?"

Mary Elizabeth said, "Harold, the results from this morning's lab tests confirm my suspicion that you are suffering from dehydration."

"And how did you reach that conclusion?" Harold asked.

Mary Elizabeth looked at her notes. "You reported that you were drinking more water than usual, and you noticed that your mind was working slower. Plus, when I first met you outside the hospital in the heat of the day on Monday, I could tell from your slow response that you were dehydrated. Here, if we do the skin test, you will see that if I pinch your skin, it takes a while to get back into shape." She reached over and pinched the back of his hand. "See? The numbers from your urine and blood work, plus all those symptoms, point to dehydration. My treatment plan is to rehydrate you with an IV bag of nine percent saline solution. That should do the trick."

Harold asked, "May I see the test results for myself?"

"Of course," Mary Elizabeth said. "Usually, I would interpret the results for my patients, but I will make an exception in your case. I assume you are perfectly capable of interpreting the numbers yourself, Dr. Merton." She smiled as she handed his chart over to him.

Harold looked sheepish as he took the chart from her. "How long have you known?"

Just then, Dr. Applegate came into the room.

Harold said, "Basil, she knows. Did you tell her?"

Dr. Applegate looked surprised. "No, Harold, I kept your confidence. Dr. Senty, how did you discover his true identity?"

"I had my suspicions after Dr. Westby told us about Mr. Merton's response to the unsuccessful blood-draw. And then Dr. Upton told me that he kept his medical records with him in Bellechester, which I found quite odd. It was Dr. Upton who told me that he is Dr. Merton, the general practitioner for the village."

Turning to Dr. Merton, she asked, "Harold, "Why did you keep your identity a secret?"

"I promise, Emme, I will tell you everything at lunch."

Dr. Applegate said, "I do believe the two of you will have quite the conversation at lunch. I imagine truth telling will be on the menu for both of you. Now that you have completed your examination, Dr. Senty, what is your diagnosis?"

Mary Elizabeth said, "Dr. Applegate, the lab results show that he is dehydrated. I am giving him a saline solution to get his body fluids back within the normal range. The sheet with the lab results is on the table if you would like to look at them."

As Dr. Applegate picked up and read the lab results, Harold said, "Basil, I agree with her diagnosis. I cannot find fault with the symptoms she observed, nor her interpretation of the test results. And I concur with her treatment plan."

"Then proceed, Dr. Senty."

Mary Elizabeth went out and brought the IV stand into the room. She then washed her hands and got everything ready. "Harold, in which hand would you like the IV?"

"Left."

Mary Elizabeth rolled the IV stand over beside his bed. "Okay, Harold, here comes the poke." She expertly inserted the needle, secured it, and wrapped gauze around so it wouldn't fall out. Then she regulated the drip, and it was done. "You should be done in about forty-five minutes." She cleaned up the table and brought his chart over. "Except for the dehydration, Harold, you are in good health. For now, it is enough just for your personal physician to keep an eye on your enlarged prostate. But I would recommend a physical exam every year or two. There, I have given you my evaluation. Now it is your turn to evaluate me. How did I do on your physical? Now remember, you said it would be an honest evaluation."

"Yes, Emme, I did promise you and Basil a fair evaluation. Personally, I would have done the exam in a different order, but your technique was sound. You promised you would explain what you were going to do, and that helped alleviate my anxiety. You were professional, and you kept the exam moving. I could not find fault. Well done. And I will take your recommendation of more frequent exams to heart. And, Basil, you were correct. She does have an excellent bedside manner."

Dr. Applegate said, "I told you she was a competent doctor."

Mary Elizabeth said, "Was this some kind of final exam for me? I can't quite figure out, Dr. Applegate, why you specified that Mr. Merton's doctor perform all his medical procedures."

Dr. Applegate said, "It was an exam for you of sorts. But Harold will explain everything at lunch. One thing puzzles me, Dr. Senty. Why did you call Dr. Upton?"

"Since we did not have his medical records, I wanted to make sure I was not missing anything;

plus I needed to know if he was current on his vaccinations."

"You have to hand it to her, Harold. She is thorough and resourceful."

"That she is, Basil. Did you teach her that?"

"No, I cannot take the credit for that. Who taught you to follow up like that, Dr. Senty?"

"No one, really. I just like to make sure I'm not missing anything. It just makes sense to me. Is there anything else I can do for you, Harold?"

"No, Emme."

"Dr. Applegate, when you are finished here, I would like to consult with you regarding another patient. I will be in the conference room."

"Yes, Dr. Senty, I will be with you in a few minutes."

"Thank you, Dr. Applegate. And, Harold, I will see you in about a half an hour to take out your IV." Mary Elizabeth left the two men alone and went to the conference room and again put up Mr. Baxter's X-rays on the scope.

After Mary Elizabeth left the room, Dr. Applegate asked, "Well, do you think you have found the young doctor you were searching for?"

"Yes, I have. But do you think she will come to Bellechester? Being American, maybe she wants to go back home. She is so competent, I am sure she would have no problem finding a position anywhere she wants. Basil, be realistic. Would she really want to come to a village in the Shropshire Hills and go into practice with an old fogey like me?"

Dr. Applegate sat down in the chair next to his friend and said, "There is only one way to find out. You must ask her. There must be some wonderful aspects to living in Bellechester. You have been happy there all these years, haven't you?"

"Well, yes, I have. But I am a simple man, and Bellechester suits me just fine. Emme is a young woman. She must have dreams and ambitions. Does she want a husband and children? I am afraid she would not find many prospects in our village."

Dr. Applegate smiled. "Now, Harold, don't overthink this. You are only offering her a job. Just be honest with her. She will have questions. Answer them truthfully. You must know by now that she will know if joining you in Bellechester is right for her."

"I just don't want her to be unhappy."

"Look, why don't you suggest a trial period? Three months? Six months? Then you can both evaluate whether it is a good fit."

"That is a splendid idea. Thank you."

"Glad to help." Dr. Applegate got up to leave.

"One last question: Where should I take her for lunch? Do you know somewhere quiet where we could have a frank conversation?"

"Why not let Dr. Senty decide? I am sure she can find a place close by that will fit the bill. Oh, before I forget. Dr. Senty will probably discharge you before lunch. You can put your suitcase in my office, and after lunch, you can walk around the city or stay in my reception area with Mrs. Stanfield until I take you home with me tonight. Caroline said she is planning something special. She is eager to see you again."

"And I her. Thank you, Basil, for everything."

"You are most welcome, Harold. And I will see you later this afternoon." Dr. Applegate left

Harold's room and joined Mary Elizabeth in the conference room.

CHAPTER 16

MR. BAXTER'S DIAGNOSIS

Mary Elizabeth had Mr. Baxter's X-rays up on the fluoroscope and was looking at them when Dr. Applegate came in the room.

"Well, Dr. Senty, what do we have here?" Dr. Applegate asked.

"It looks like Mr. Baxter has fluid building up outside his lungs. He says it hurts when he breathes. I would like to perform a pleurocentesis to drain the excess fluid. That should help his breathing and relieve any pain or discomfort he is experiencing."

"Yes, I agree. Where are you thinking to insert the needle?"

Mary Elizabeth pointed on the X-ray. "I think if I go in here above this rib, I should be able to drain the fluid easily."

"Yes, that looks like a good spot. Do you feel confident in performing the procedure?"

"Yes, but even though I have successfully performed several of these procedures before, I would like one of our senior pulmonologists to be present, just in case. With Mr. Baxter's leg in a cast, it will be a challenge to get him properly positioned for the procedure, but I am certain we can do it. I will see to it that his pain medication is adjusted again so he will be able to tolerate all the movement."

"When would you like to do the procedure?"

"Later this afternoon, about four."

"Would you mind if I had some of the other junior doctors come and watch the procedure?"

"No, of course not. I will be sure to talk to Mr. Baxter about it, but I do not believe he will have any objections."

"Very good, Dr. Senty. Put your orders in, and I will arrange for the pulmonologist."

"Thank you, Dr. Applegate."

As he walked out the door, he said, "My pleasure."

Mary Elizabeth studied the X-ray for a few more minutes, wrote down notes for herself, and then headed for the nurses' station to write up her orders. After handing them to Matron Hartly, she headed down to speak to Mr. Baxter. Knocking on his door, she walked in and said, "Good morning, Mr. Baxter."

"Good morning, Dr. Senty. I wasn't expecting to see you until this afternoon."

"What I came to talk with you about are your X-rays. They show that fluid is building up outside your lungs. That is why it is difficult for you to breathe and why your lungs hurt."

"That is strange. Fluid on the outside of my lungs? What can be done about it?"

"We perform a procedure called a pleurocentesis to drain the excess fluid."

"Does that mean another operation?"

"No, you will be awake for this procedure. I will be inserting a needle in your back between your ribs. The needle will draw out the fluid."

Mr. Baxter shuddered. "Sounds painful."

"Yes, it does sound painful. But here is what we do. I will numb up a spot on your back with a local anesthetic, and you will not feel a thing, I promise. Then I insert a larger needle to draw out the fluid. Samples will be sent to the lab, which will tell us all sorts of things so we can rule out more serious diseases. After all the fluid is drained out, I remove the needle and put a bandage on it, and that is all. Immediately, you will feel relief. No more lung pain or difficulty breathing."

"Well, that part sounds good. Will you be the one performing the procedure?"

"Yes."

"I trust you, Dr. Senty. If that is what you say needs to be done, then let's do it."

"Would you mind if some of our younger doctors came and watched the procedure?"

"Being a student myself, how could I refuse?"

"Great. Thank you, Mr. Baxter. I love your positive attitude. The procedure is scheduled for this afternoon at four. Now before I go, do you have any questions for me?"

"I can't think of any."

"You rest up, and I will see you then."

"Thank you, Doctor."

Mary Elizabeth left Mr. Baxter's room and walked up to the nurses' station. She finished writing up her notes on Mr. Baxter and then handed Matron Hartly his chart. "Matron, could I have Mr. Merton's file? I am going to begin writing up his discharge papers. Once his IV is finished, he should be ready to go."

Matron Hartly answered, "Here you go. I am going to miss him. He is such a dear man."

"Yes, he is. May I have a blood pressure cuff? I will take another reading." Mary Elizabeth took his chart and the blood pressure cuff and walked back to Mr. Merton's room. She knocked on his door and walked in.

Harold was working on a crossword puzzle.

"Harold, how are you doing?" she asked.

"Just fine, Emme. Is the IV done?"

Mary Elizabeth looked at the IV bottle. "Just a few more drops." She put down her supplies. "Mind if I take another reading while we are waiting?"

"No, go ahead." Harold was still absorbed in his puzzle.

Mary Elizabeth fitted the cuff on his arm. "Okay, Harold, here comes the squeeze. One twelve over seventy-eight. Very good."

"Yes, that sounds about right," Harold said.

"And now you are finished." She shut off the flow, removed the needle, and bandaged his hand. "There, all done. I am going to write up my notes and your discharge papers. Do you need any assistance walking to the bathroom or getting dressed?"

"No, I will be fine. Thank you."

"Just remember to take it easy. Sit on the side of the bed for a few minutes before you stand up."

"Yes, Emme." Harold smiled. "I will remember."

"I'll be back in a few minutes." She walked out of his room and into the lounge. She sat down at the table and began writing up her notes for his chart. She remembered to write out two copies: one for Dr. Upton and one for Harold to keep in his record at Bellechester. She finished writing his discharge papers and again put one in his hospital file and one for Harold to take with him. When she was done, she put her lab coat in her locker and grabbed her purse and Harold's file.

Mary Elizabeth walked to the nurses' station. "Matron Hartly, here is Mr. Merton's file. Could you mail this copy of his hospital stay to Dr. Upton in Glendale? I have his discharge papers and will be going over them with him. Could you please call an orderly with a wheelchair to take him to the hospital entrance?"

"Yes, Doctor."

"After I finish with Mr. Merton, I will be going on a long lunch. I will be back on the floor after three."

"Well, good for you," Matron Hartly said. She then picked up the phone and called for the orderly.

Mary Elizabeth walked down to room 712 and knocked on the door.

Harold called out, "Come in."

Mary Elizabeth walked in and found Harold dressed, sitting on the bed with his closed suitcase.

"All set to go, Harold?" Mary Elizabeth asked. "Matron Hartly will be mailing a copy of your medical record to Dr. Upton, and a copy in this envelope is for your record in Bellechester. If we can take a moment, I'll go over your discharge papers with you."

"Of course," Harold said.

"You were admitted on Monday to receive a physical examination. In the course of the exam, you were found to be suffering from dehydration. A nine percent saline solution was administered intravenously. You should make sure you drink plenty of fluids to keep hydrated. You should make an appointment with your primary doctor for a physical in another year when he can check on your prostate. There, have I forgotten anything?"

"As usual, you are very thorough, Emme," Harold said.

"An orderly is going to take you in a wheel-chair downstairs. I will meet you outside."

As she got up to go, there was a knock on the door, and an orderly came in with the wheelchair.

"Your chariot awaits," Mary Elizabeth said as the orderly got Harold situated.

Harold held his suitcase in his lap. "If you please, could you take me to Dr. Applegate's of-fice? I am going to leave my suitcase with him while I go to lunch."

The orderly said, "Of course, sir." With that, they headed to Dr. Applegate's office. The order-ly left the suitcase with Mrs. Stanfield. A lift ride later, they were on the main floor. The orderly expertly maneuvered Harold in the wheelchair through the lobby and out a side door. Soon they were at the public sidewalk. "End of the line, sir," the orderly said cheerfully as he helped Har-old up.

"Thank you," Harold said. It was cloudy out, but even so, he squinted until he got used to the brightness of the day. True to her word, Mary

Elizabeth was waiting for him at the end of the sidewalk.

"Well, now the only thing left for us to do is go have lunch. I am starved. Where are we going?" Mary Elizabeth said.

"I don't know any of the eating establishments around here. Basil said that you could recommend a place. I only ask that it be somewhere quiet. It seems that you and I have some important matters to discuss," Harold said.

"Oh my. That sounds serious." Mary Elizabeth looked at her watch. "If you liked the sandwich you had on Monday, we could go to Little Italy. Alex can set us up in a quiet spot where we can talk. How does that sound?"

"That sounds wonderful. Yes, I did enjoy that sandwich, and if the rest of the food is that good, then that will be a real treat," Harold said. "Being cooped up in the hospital for the past few days, I realized how much I had taken for granted. That experience has given me a deeper sense of gratitude for the ability to go where I want and when I want. I have developed much more empathy for my patients. Yes, Emme, there were many important lessons learned."

CHAPTER 17

LITTLE ITALY

The restaurant was just down the street from the hospital. Little Italy took up three shop spaces. Mary Elizabeth led Harold through the door. Immediately, the warm smell of baked bread and fresh tomato sauce enveloped them.

"*Buongiorno*, Alex," Mary Elizabeth called out to the young man sitting behind the counter.

"*Ah, buongiorno, Signorina Maria Elisabetta.* Have you brought *un amico* with you today?" Alex asked.

"*Sì.* I would like to introduce to you Dr. Harold Merton."

Harold offered his hand. His hospital bracelet dangled about his wrist. "Very pleased to make your acquaintance, Alex."

Alex shook his hand vigorously. "Always pleased to meet a friend of *Maria Elisabetta's.*"

Mary Elizabeth, seeing Harold's bracelet, asked, "Alex, do you have scissors that we could use to snip off his bracelet?"

"*Sì.* Right here," Alex pulled out a pair of scissors from behind his counter.

"*Grazie,*" Mary Elizabeth said as she cut the bracelet off. She handed the scissors back to Alex.

Harold took the bracelet and stuffed it in his jacket pocket. "A souvenir from my trip," he said.

"*Un tavolo per due?*" Alex asked.

"*Sì. Un tavolo in un posto tranquillo, per favore?*" Mary Elizabeth said.

"*Capisco,*" Alex replied. Since the lunch hour was winding down, the restaurant was mostly empty. The few diners who remained were lingering over their desserts and tea. Alex led Mary Elizabeth and Harold to a table toward the back. There were no other diners in that entire section.

"*Grazie,*" Mary Elizabeth said.

Alex pulled out the chair for her, and Mary Elizabeth sat down at a square table with a red-and-white checkered tablecloth. A small bouquet of fresh daisies and snapdragons were set in a green glass vase in the middle of the table. Harold sat down, and Alex handed them their menus.

"What is *tua madre* cooking today?" Mary Elizabeth asked.

Alex answered with a smile, "Mama made a pan of lasagna this morning."

Mary Elizabeth said, *"Fantastico!"*

Alex laughed. *"Maria Elisabetta,* your grasp of the Italian language is"—Alex kissed his fingertips and flung them out—*"molto buono.* May I start you out with a nice red wine?"

Mary Elizabeth sighed. "I would love it, but I can't today because I have to go back to work. Just my usual, water with lemon for me. But, Harold, you could have a glass of wine, if you promise to drink plenty of water to keep hydrated this afternoon. I do want you to have an authentic Italian meal, and the red wine goes so well with the food."

Harold smiled. "All right, Emme. why not?"

Alex turned to Mary Elizabeth. "*Sei Emme?*"

Mary Elizabeth said, "*Si*. Emme is my nickname."

Alex said, "Very good, sir. I will bring you a glass of our house red."

Mary Elizabeth and Harold took a moment to look over the menus. "I have no idea what to order. What do you suggest?" Harold asked.

"Alex said that his mother made lasagna today. That is one of my favorite dishes. Would you like to try that? We could have garlic bread and a Caprese salad with the lasagna," Mary Elizabeth said.

"Sounds good to me," Harold said. He looked around. Colorful scenes from an Italian village decorated the walls of the restaurant. "I feel like we are actually in Italy."

"Isn't this great? I come here often, especially when I want to take a break from the hospital. I imagine myself in some sunny Italian village near a vineyard instead of in rainy, dreary London. And the food is just wonderful. So tasty."

"We have nothing like this back home. This will be a real adventure."

By that time, Alex was back with the drinks. Harold relayed to him their order. When they were alone again, he said, "This is very nice. I am so glad that we could have this lunch together. Remember, this time, it is my treat. I do want to repay you for the kindness you showed me last Monday."

"Last Monday," Mary Elizabeth repeated. "Last Monday seems like a lifetime ago."

"I keep thinking about how we met, and I can't help but wonder why you stopped to help me. No one else gave me a second look."

"I was on my way to a late lunch, actually, I was on my way here, and I saw you on the sidewalk with your suitcase, looking up at the hospital. The look on your face of half-fear and half-awe reminded me of myself when I saw Mother of Mercy Hospital for the first time. You just looked like you needed some reassurance that everything was going to be fine and that you were indeed in the right place."

"I probably shouldn't tell you this, but when I first heard your voice, I thought you were an angel."

"An angel?" Mary Elizabeth laughed. "Really? Oh, Harold, your heat exhaustion was worse than I'd thought."

"Seriously, Emme," Harold continued, "in many ways, you were an answer to a prayer. Several prayers, as a matter of fact."

Just then, Alex set their salad plates in front of them. He quickly returned with the Caprese salad and garlic bread. *"Buon appetito!"*

"Thank you, Alex," Harold said.

Mary Elizabeth said, *"Grazie."*

"The food looks delicious, almost too pretty to eat," Harold said as he passed Mary Elizabeth the plate with the tomato slices, basil leaves, and mozzarella cheese artfully arranged.

"You're right. Almost. But I am starved. It was a busy morning," Mary Elizabeth said as she filled her plate.

Harold teased her, "Yes, you had to give an old man a physical this morning. I hear he really put you through your paces."

"Yes, he did." Mary Elizabeth smiled. "Harold, why did you come all the way to London just to get a physical exam? Couldn't Dr. Upton have given you one in Glendale? You wouldn't have had to brave the heat or a long train journey or spend three days in a hospital."

"As usual, Emme, your deductive skills are spot-on. Coming here for a physical was actually a ruse of sorts. I came to test Basil's fourth-year junior doctors."

"For what purpose? Was Dr. Applegate in on it too?"

"It was my idea to hide the fact that I was a doctor. I didn't want any special treatment. Basil went along with it. I just needed to view his fourth-years from a patient's perspective. That is why he specified that you young doctors do all the medical procedures on me."

"But, by this time," Mary Elizabeth said, "all of us are fully certified doctors and are members of The Royal College of General Practitioners."

"True. As you know, practicing medicine is not only about skill. It is also how you relate to the patient. A piece of paper wouldn't tell me that. I wanted to experience your bedside manner for myself."

"I hate to sound like a broken record, but why go through all that? Were you sent from the National Health Service?"

"No, nothing like that."

Alex appeared with their main course. As he set the plates down in front of them, Harold said, "Thank you, Alex. This looks delicious."

Alex laughed. "In Italy, we have an expression: '*Si mangia prima con gli occhi*,' which means in your language, 'You eat first with your eyes.' I guarantee that it will taste as good as it looks. Have you enjoyed your salad and bread?"

"Oh, very much. I can see why Emme recommended this place."

Mary Elizabeth said, "This food is delicious as always. Please give my compliments to your mother."

Alex smiled. "*Grazie. Buon appetito!*" He left them to enjoy their meal.

Harold said, "Emme, before I tell you the real reason for my trip to London, I need to ask you a question. It is rather personal. May I?"

Mary Elizabeth answered, "Of course."

"Basil tells me that your time at Mother of Mercy Hospital is coming to an end on Friday. What are your plans?"

"I am spending the weekend as a houseguest of Dr. and Mrs. Stuart Harrington II in London. They are the parents of one of my colleagues. They have hosted me as well as Dr. Ruhan Batra for all the holidays these past four years. We refer to them as our London family. They are throwing a party for their son, Stuart, and all of our cohort on Saturday evening."

"That sounds like the perfect way to finish your time together. Those junior doctor cohorts can become pretty close," Harold said.

"Yes, we have become good friends. It will be strange not to see them after Sunday. Was Dr. Applegate in your cohort? Is that where you met him?" Mary Elizabeth asked.

"Basil and I have been friends ever since university. We were together all the way through our junior doctor program. Hard to believe, but our friendship spans over four decades."

"No wonder Dr. Applegate was so concerned about the care you received."

Harold smiled and said, "Yes, that had something to do with it, but that was not the only reason. Now, Emme, what are your plans after the weekend? Your long-term plans?"

Harold watched as her usual sunny disposition faded. Mary Elizabeth's shoulders slumped as she dropped her eyes and toyed with her water glass. Speaking in a serious tone, she said, "I had a plan. It was a good one, or so I thought." She paused and looked directly at Harold. "You see, I had secured a fellowship at a hospital in Boston, Massachusetts. They teach a special program in gerontology. Boston is still twelve hundred miles from home, but at least I would be in the United States. I am certified to practice medicine in England, but my medical license in Minnesota has lapsed. So, while spending the year working on my American Board of Medical Specialties, I was also going to work on my Minnesota recertification. After that, I had hoped to practice medicine in my home state of Minnesota." She added with a sigh, "It has been so long since I have been home."

Harold said, "That does sound like a very good plan."

Mary Elizabeth said sadly, "It was. I received a letter yesterday saying that the hospital has rescinded my fellowship. They don't want me."

"But why?" Harold asked.

"They say it is because too many of the male doctors did not want to work with a female doctor. I thought five years was enough time for everything to blow over, but I guess it wasn't," Mary Elizabeth said quietly.

"What do you mean?"

"When I was interning at Bentley Hospital, back in Minnesota, there was a very well-known doctor, Dr. Anderson, who enjoyed preying upon young and innocent nurses and female doctors. He even got several of them pregnant. It was like a sport with him. The hospital made excuses for his behavior. They didn't want to tarnish his reputation, nor their own, so they just turned a blind eye. I had heard the stories, but I couldn't believe a doctor could behave that way. Until, that is, he tried it with me."

Harold reached across the table and held her hand. "Oh my, Emme, we don't have to talk about this. I didn't mean to pry."

Mary Elizabeth gave a slight smile, "No, it's all right. I want to tell you the whole story. Well, I don't know if I mentioned it, but I am the second oldest of ten children. I have six younger brothers. One of them joined the U.S. Marines after high school. Before I left to go to medical school in the big city, my father insisted my brother give me a crash course in self-defense. He taught me well. When Dr. Anderson tried something, my instincts kicked in, and I am afraid he bore the fruits of my brother's military training."

Harold asked, "What happened?"

"He had invited me to his office, as I was going to assist on one of his surgeries. We finished our business, and then he grabbed me and tried to force himself on me. I kneed him hard in the groin. He was off balance, so I pushed him hard. He fell back and crashed into a glass coffee table. I got out of his office as fast as I could and immediately reported it to security. After Dr. Anderson recovered from his injuries, he threatened to get me thrown out of the program. But by this time, several of us had enough information on him, so we fought back. We found a young lawyer to represent us. We had taped conversations and depositions that showed a long pattern of his criminal behavior. Even when faced with all the evidence, the hospital still refused to do anything about it."

"That must have been demoralizing," Harold said.

"It was, but not wholly unexpected. Our next move was to contact a newspaper reporter. He had his own team of investigators, and they not only corroborated our information but also found tons of new information on Dr. Anderson. The hospital tried to kill the story, but the newspaper stood their ground. They ran the story: the doctor, the cover-up by the hospital, and the culture of harassment in the medical field. The story turned into a series that ran in the paper for over a week. In fact, several of the national newspapers picked up the story as well. The reporters and the paper won all sorts of awards for their work on the story. Now, Beaver Falls, Minnesota, is really a very small city, more like a town. Soon the scandal was all anyone could talk about for weeks. Finally, it was the hospital board of directors that that forced Dr. Anderson to retire. The chair was the granddaughter of one of the founding Bentley families. She was a real force of nature who did not want the legacy of her family tarnished by a doctor who could not keep his pants zipped. Our lecherous doctor did not get all the justice he deserved, but at least he was banned from the hospital, and his medical license was revoked. What happened to him served as a warning to any doctor that would use his position for personal gratification. I do believe we helped to change the culture of that hospital. The female staff is now respected for their professional contributions. I feel good about that. But I am afraid that this all came at a terrible cost."

Harold asked, "What do you mean?"

"The hospital quietly forced all the nurses who were named in the newspaper article to quit their jobs at the hospital. Besides giving them a 'separation' bonus based on their tenure, the hospital helped them find alternative employment out of town. In exchange, the nurses signed an agreement that they would not talk about their experiences ever again."

"Oh my. And the female doctors? What happened to them?" Harold asked.

Mary Elizabeth gave a wry laugh. "You mean me? Harold, don't you know that interns are expendable? Since I was just there for the year anyway, they didn't even bother with me at all. However, Dr. Anderson became obsessed with focusing his revenge on me."

Harold could not believe what he was hearing. "What did he do?"

Mary Elizabeth said, "Dr. Anderson enjoyed an international reputation for his groundbreaking work in brain surgery. Consequently, he was very well connected to all the teaching hospitals in the United States. He did his darnedest to get me blackballed in every residency program in the United States and Canada. I was labeled as a troublemaker who was out to ruin every male doctor's career. No residency program would touch me with a ten-foot pole. But there was no way that he was going to keep me from my dream. I am a fighter. I had come too far." Mary Elizabeth looked at Harold. "I don't give up that easily."

"Yes, I have witnessed some of your tenacity," Harold said.

"Harold, haven't you ever wondered why I would come all the way to London to finish my training?" Mary Elizabeth asked.

Harold thought for a moment. Then he said, "I guess, now that you mention it, I was curious as to how an American ended up in Basil's program."

"One of my supervising physicians reached out to his international connections. He had met Dr. Applegate at a conference here in London. He wrote to Dr. Applegate on my behalf and sent him my academic record and all my references. I will be forever grateful to him for advocating for me and to Dr. Applegate for taking a chance on me."

"Remember, Emme," Harold said, "Basil may have given you a chance, but look what you did with it. That was all you."

"Harold, you are too kind. I may have won the battle five years ago, but I am afraid Dr. Anderson has won the war."

"What do you mean?"

She just shrugged and forced a smile. "Originally, I had planned to fly to Boston on Sunday to begin my post-residency fellowship. Two weeks ago, I gave notice at my boardinghouse, and my landlady has already found another boarder. Dr. Applegate told me not to worry, that things will work out. But come Monday, I have no job and no place to live. I suppose I could just fly to Boston on Sunday and then take a train back home to Minnesota." Tears began to form in her eyes and started running down her cheeks. "Because I have been away from Minnesota for over five years, I would have to go through the medical license certification process again before I could practice medicine. I just can't go home yet without a job."

The dam broke. All the emotions that Mary Elizabeth had bottled up inside her spilled out. Her chest began heaving, and she had a difficult time speaking in between sobs. "I . . . . I just . . . don't know . . . what I . . . am going to do." She put her head down and went searching in her purse. Because her tears were blurring her vision, she could not find what she was looking for right away. Her purse searching became more frantic.

"Emme?" Harold said softly. "Emme. Emme, please. Take this." He reached across the table with a neatly ironed white linen handkerchief in his hand. "I am sorry, Emme. I didn't mean to upset you. Please. Don't cry."

Through her tears, she said, "I'm sorry. I shouldn't be spoiling our nice lunch by burdening you with my problems."

"Emme, look at me," Harold said firmly. "I feel privileged that you shared your story with me. I think that you are a very brave and extraordinary woman. And you are a very fine doctor. I don't want you to ever think that Dr. Anderson has destroyed your dream of becoming a practicing physician. Why, any doctor would be proud to have you on their staff. I know I would. And you must believe what Basil told you."

Mary Elizabeth got herself under control once again. She dried her tears and blew her nose. "I am trying. But the time is growing short. At this point, I have no idea where to even begin to search for a position."

Harold said, "Now, don't be unhappy. I have it on good authority that you will be receiving a job offer shortly."

"A job? Really? Where? With whom?"

Harold sat back in his chair and patted his rotund middle. "My, that was a wonderful meal. Thank you for suggesting this place. You are going to have to roll me out of here. What's for dessert?"

"Oh no you don't," Mary Elizabeth said. "You aren't leaving me dangling by changing the subject. Tell me."

Alex came and took away their dinner plates. Mary Elizabeth asked, "Alex, what dessert would you recommend for my friend for his first Italian meal?"

Alex looked at Harold and smiled. "Of course, he must finish it off with tiramisu."

"Certainly, and I'll have your lemon panna cotta. Thanks, Alex."

When they were alone again, Mary Elizabeth leaned over the table and whispered, "Harold Merton, don't you dare leave me in suspense any longer. Now, please tell me. How do you know I will be offered a job?"

"All right, I will tell you. But I really thought that by using your deductive powers," Harold said, pointing to his temple, "you would have figured everything out by now."

Mary Elizabeth said, "I guess I am not as bright as you'd thought."

Alex appeared with their desserts. "Will there be anything else this afternoon?"

Harold answered, "Could you bring us two teas, please?"

"Of course," Alex said.

Harold attacked his dessert with gusto. "The reason I know you are going to be offered a job this afternoon is because I am going to offer you one," he said matter-of-factly.

"I don't want you to do that because you feel sorry for me," Mary Elizabeth said as she jutted out her chin. Her expression was identical to the one Harold had seen earlier that morning in his hospital room.

"I am not doing it out of pity," Harold said. He then turned all his attention to his dessert. "Oh my, this dessert is wonderful. I have never tasted anything like it before."

"I'm glad you are enjoying it," Mary Elizabeth said. "Now, why are you offering me a job?"

Harold said, "I should start at the beginning. Emme, the real reason for my trip to London and to Mother of Mercy Hospital was that I was on a mission to find a young doctor to join me in my practice. I am getting older, and the town is growing. The doctor I am looking for not only has to be knowledgeable but also extremely skillful. My practice is small. I have a very efficient receptionist and bookkeeper who manages the business side of things. But there is no nurse. So the doctor I choose must be competent to perform all medical procedures."

"Is that why Dr. Applegate put that note in your chart?" Mary Elizabeth asked.

"Yes. Basil assigned Dr. Westby to my case because, at the time, he was the only one from your cohort who did not already have any employment plans. But he turned out to be neither skillful nor competent. And his bedside manner, well," Harold said as he finished his dessert, "let's just say it left a lot to be desired. There is no way that I would ever let him anywhere near my patients. No, he was not right for Bellechester."

Harold put his fork down on his empty plate and looked up at Mary Elizabeth. "But you, dear Emme, passed those tests with flying colors. Plus, you have an excellent way of making patients feel comfortable around you. Besides, having grown up in a small town, you have experience with rural living. As you must know, not everyone is suited to country life. All things considered, I think you would be a perfect fit for Bellechester. Will you come and join me in my practice?"

CHAPTER 18

CONSIDERATIONS

Alex reappeared with a large tray that held a tea service and set everything down on their table. Harold said, "Alex, your dessert was out of this world."

Mary Elizabeth said, "Yes, Alex, everything was delicious as usual."

"*Grazie.*" Alex put the check down by Harold. "Take your time. No rush. You can pay me at the front on your way out."

Harold said, "Thank you, Alex."

Alex left the table, and they were alone again.

Mary Elizabeth sipped her tea. She was silent for a long time. Finally, she put down her teacup and said, "Okay. Before I give you my final answer, I have some questions."

Harold smiled. "Yes, Basil said you would have questions. Ask away."

"Do you think the people of Bellechester would accept a woman doctor?"

"I will be honest. It will take folks a while to warm up to you. But you shouldn't take it personally. They treat all newcomers the same way. I am sure that once they get to know you, they will take to you. When they see that I have trust in you, they will come around. I will even ask my friend Matt, Father Evenson, to help too. He is very well respected in the village. Folks listen to what he says."

"Yes, I would love to meet your friend Father Evenson. Harold, you know that my faith is very important to me. So the fact that there is a Catholic church in town is a point in your favor."

"I didn't know this was a contest," Harold said, laughing.

Mary Elizabeth smiled. "Well, right now, it is. I have to see if things add up in my head."

"As you wish. Next question."

"How big an area does your practice cover?"

"Besides the town of Bellechester, I have patients on some of the outlying farms. And then there is Brantwell Manor and a few other estates in the area. And, of course, the two Benedictine monasteries. All told, I think I cover about six square miles in the southwestern part of the county."

"So it would be beneficial for me to have my own car?"

"Well, yes, eventually. But at first, I will take all the house calls for the outer areas. Your help would be appreciated in taking care of the patients that come to the clinic and all the calls in the village."

"Where would I live? Is there someone who would take in a boarder?"

Mary Elizabeth's question took Harold by surprise. "You mean you wouldn't live in the doctor's residence with me?"

"Harold!" Mary Elizabeth lowered her voice. "How would that go over with the villagers? I know that it is 1959 and all, but still, how respectable would it be for two of us, single doctors, one male and one female, to be sharing the same house?"

Harold furrowed his brow and sipped his tea. "I guess I just assumed that since the clinic is attached to the doctor's residence, that the new doctor would live there with me." He took another sip of tea. He looked at her thoughtfully. "I suppose you being a woman complicates things."

Mary Elizabeth smiled at Harold's naïveté. "Yes, my being a woman does complicate things just a tad."

"But don't you think it would all work out? I don't know if I mentioned it, but the office and residence are quite large. The office has two fully equipped exam rooms, a pharmacy area, small laboratory, and an X-ray room. In the residence, my bedroom is on the main floor, but there is a very spacious second floor that has five good-size bedrooms and a bathroom. That is where I thought you would have your room. You could make one of the other bedrooms into a sitting area or a study or anything you wanted. To be honest, I never go up there. Everything I need is on the first floor. The common rooms downstairs would be the dining room, kitchen, and sitting room. I have a housekeeper who comes and fixes my meals and does the laundry and the cleaning. Her name is Mrs. Duggan, and she has been with me for many years. If we talked to her and raised her wages, I am sure she would take care of your needs too."

"Oh, does she live there with you?"

"No, she is not a live-in housekeeper like Father Evenson has. Mrs. Duggan has her own place in the village."

"If she were a live-in housekeeper, that would make things easier. I think that the matter of my housing needs more thought." Mary Elizabeth sipped her tea.

"As usual, you are right, Emme. I certainly do not want to compromise your reputation. But I am sure once you see my residence and the office for yourself, you will see that it all will work out." He paused as he sipped his tea. "Yes, I will even see about adding a telephone extension upstairs." He looked up at her excitedly.

"Before you go through all that trouble and expense, I should probably look the place over."

"Of course. If the residence does not meet your standards, I am sure we could come up with an alternative living situation for you."

Mary Elizabeth set down her teacup. "Harold, I don't mean to be difficult. If it were just up to me, living in the doctor's residence would be fine. In fact, it sounds like it would be very convenient. I am really not that fussy about my living quarters. It's just that I don't want to give the villagers any more ammunition to use against me. Let's face it. It is going to be an uphill battle to get them to accept a woman doctor who also happens to be an American. That is two strikes against me right off the bat. And in our American game of baseball, three strikes and you are out." She looked at her watch. The time was 3:04 p.m. "Harold, I am afraid I need to get back to the hospital soon. I am doing a pleurocentesis at four today."

"You know how to perform that procedure? Emme, I am impressed. Would you mind if I came and observed?" Harold asked as he finished his tea.

"No, not at all. Dr. Applegate and some of the junior doctors will be coming too. The more the merrier. Are you ready to go?" Emme asked as she began to gather her purse and gloves.

"But, Emme, you haven't given me your answer."

"I haven't given you my answer because I haven't made up my mind yet."

"Do you have any more questions? Is there something more I need to tell you?"

Mary Elizabeth got up from the table and began putting on her gloves. "Harold, this is a very big decision. I just need a little more time to carefully consider everything. But I will not leave you dangling." She looked him straight in the eye. "I promise that after I finish with Mr. Baxter's procedure, we will sit down and talk again. You will have my answer before you leave for your dinner with Dr. Applegate and his wife. Will that be acceptable?"

Harold stood up. "Of course. I realize that deciding your future is a big step. But please know that I would not have offered you the position if I didn't think you were the right person for the job and for Bellechester."

Mary Elizabeth smiled. "Thank you, Harold. I appreciate your confidence in me."

By this time, they had reached the front of the restaurant. Alex was behind the counter.

Mary Elizabeth said, "*Grazie* to you and your mother for a most wonderful lunch."

Harold said, "Alex, this was my first Italian meal, but I know it will not be my last. Everything was so delicious. And the dessert was the best I had ever tasted. *Grazie*."

Alex said, "Please do come back and bring your friends. *Buona giornata*."

"*Buona giornata* to you too," said Mary Elizabeth as they exited the restaurant.

As they strolled back to the hospital, Harold said, "I wish I could take Little Italy back to Bellechester with me. The food was wonderful."

"Yes, I am going to miss that place too. Alex is teaching me Italian. He and his mother have been so kind to me. They have adopted me into their family. Whenever I needed to get away from the hospital, they were there for me. They helped to keep me grounded."

"Grounded?" Harold asked. "What do you mean?"

"They remind me to appreciate the simple things in life, such as good food, family, and friends. They embrace life. And in their world, there is always a place at the table for you or for me. As doctors, we have the heavy responsibility to *do* for people. Our actions or inaction can mean the difference between life and death for the people who put themselves in our hands. I find that the responsibility can weigh me down. I can turn in on myself. My world can get pretty small. But when I go to Little Italy, Alex and his family's warm hospitality reminds me that I don't always have to *do*, I can just be. I relax. I can enjoy the simple things like good food and a good glass of wine. Spending time in their company is like spending time with my own family. It renews my spirit and reminds me of who I am and what I want to bring to the work I do. Does that make sense?"

"Yes, Emme, I understand. I did feel like I was in a different world, and it was nice and relaxing. I can see why you enjoy going there. Thank you for sharing that experience with me. I will remember it for a long time."

CHAPTER 19

$\mathcal{G}$ONE TOO FAR

As they entered the hospital and rode the lift to the seventh floor, Mary Elizabeth asked, "Harold, where in Bellechester do you go when you need to get away and revive your spirit?"

"I take my dog, and we spend time up in the Hills. I would like to show you the Shropshire Hills, Emme. To me, it is the most beautiful place on earth. You can lose yourself and find yourself there, all in the same visit."

"Sounds lovely."

The lift doors opened, and as they walked by the nurses' station, they noticed that the shift was changing. The station was crowded as the nurses were conversing with each other. Off to the side, Matron Hartly was speaking with Matron Carruthers. When she saw Dr. Senty, she called out, "How was your lunch?"

Harold and Mary Elizabeth stopped. Mary Elizabeth said, "We went to Little Italy."

Harold added, "The food was the best I ever tasted."

Matron Hartly said, "I'm glad you both enjoyed yourselves." Then she turned and continued her conversation with Matron Carruthers. Matron Carruthers was aghast.

"Dr. Senty was out to lunch with one of her patients!"

Matron Hartly said, "Dr. Senty discharged Mr. Merton earlier, so technically he wasn't her patient anymore. Dr. Senty is free to go to lunch with whomever she pleases. I don't see the harm in it. And I fail to see how this is any of your concern."

Matron Carruthers made no reply, but she continued to watch Mary Elizabeth and Harold.

Harold and Mary Elizabeth walked down the hall. When they got to the junior doctors' lounge, Harold and Mary Elizabeth stopped. She said, "This is where I leave you. I will be doing the pleurocentesis in Mr. Baxter's room, number 723. I will see you there."

"Room 723," Harold repeated loudly. "Thanks again for letting me watch the procedure." Harold continued down the hall to wait in Dr. Applegate's office.

Matron Carruthers turned to Matron Hartly. "Did you hear that? Dr. Senty invited Mr. Merton to watch a procedure on another patient. That is highly irregular. No, Dr. Senty has gone too far this time. Dr. Applegate must hear about this."

"Lilian, just let it go. Dr. Applegate is also bringing some of the junior doctors to watch Mr. Baxter's procedure. He will be there. He will see that Mr. Merton is also present. Dr. Applegate can deal with the situation without any help from you."

"If you ask me, Dr. Senty has Dr. Applegate wrapped around her little finger. He lets her get away with far too much around here. Someone has to open his eyes."

"Really? And you think that someone should be you? I don't know why you have it in for Dr. Senty. I don't see that Dr. Applegate treats her any differently from the other doctors. In any case, Dr. Senty and the other fourth-years will be leaving on Friday anyway."

"Well, I can see that Dr. Senty has worked her voodoo on you too. Rules and regulations must be followed. No, it is my duty to report such improper behavior to Dr. Applegate."

Seeing that nothing she said had gotten through to Matron Carruthers, Matron Hartly said, "Since you won't listen to sense, do as you wish. My shift is done. I'm going home." She left the floor.

Alone with her thoughts, Matron Carruthers was getting angrier by the minute. Unable to concentrate on any of her duties, she could not restrain herself any longer. She asked Nurse Daly to cover for her at the desk. Getting up a full head of steam, Matron Carruthers marched down the hall, opened the outer door to Dr.

Applegate's office, strode right up to Mrs. Stanfield, and said in her too-loud voice, "I need to see Dr. Applegate at once!"

Glancing to see whether Dr. Applegate was on the phone, Mrs. Stanfield rose and began to move toward the door. Speaking calmly, she said, "I'll check if he can see you."

Impatient at the seemingly slow response of Mrs. Stanfield, Matron Carruthers called out, "Don't bother," as she pushed past her and opened the door herself. "Dr. Applegate, I must see you."

The abrupt entrance of Matron Carruthers startled Dr. Applegate. He dropped his pen and sat up straight in his chair.

Mrs. Stanfield, finally wedging her way between Matron Carruthers and the door, said, "My apologies, Doctor, I couldn't stop her."

Dr. Applegate, in his usual calm, understated way, said, "It's all right, Mrs. Stanfield. I would ask you to come in, Matron Carruthers, but I see you are already here. Please, sit down." He pointed to the chair in front of his desk. "Thank you, Mrs. Stanfield, that will be all."

Mrs. Stanfield left the room, closing the door behind her.

Inside his office, Dr. Applegate asked, "And now, what brings you to my office today?"

Sitting on the edge of the chair, she said in a loud voice, "This time, Dr. Senty has gone too far!"

"Ah yes, Dr. Senty. I should have guessed. Here, let me get a fresh piece of paper so I can add it to the file." Dr. Applegate reached into his drawer and pulled out a clean sheet of paper. He opened another drawer and pulled up a file folder bulging with papers of all sizes.

"Well, I am glad to see that you are keeping a file on her."

"Yes, I have all your reports on Dr. Senty right here," he said as he patted the plump file. "Now, what has she done today?"

Matron Carruthers said in her too-loud voice, "She went out to lunch with one of her patients."

She was about to go on, but Dr. Applegate held up his hand, which stopped her. "Just to clarify for the file, which patient?"

"Why, Mr. Merton, of course. She has been after that poor man from the day he arrived. She has showered him with attention . . . visiting him, giving him back rubs, laughing and joking with him, and goodness knows what else. She has broken every medical ethical standard in the book. And then they go out to lunch together. And that isn't even the worst of it."

Dr. Applegate was busy writing down her complaints. Matron Carruthers waited until he stopped and looked up. "There is more?" he asked.

"Oh yes. Dr. Senty brought him back up to the floor. She didn't even try to hide the fact that they were out together. The worst part is that she invited Mr. Merton to watch her do a procedure on another patient. That just goes beyond the pale."

"Again, to clarify for the file, do you happen to know what procedure and which patient?"

Matron Carruthers replied, "She invited him to watch her do the pleurocentesis on Mr. Baxter."

"I see. Is there anything else?"

"Isn't that enough? Dr. Applegate, this situation with Dr. Senty has gone on long enough. It is high time you did something about it. I am afraid drastic measures must be taken. And taken soon before her behavior escalates even further."

"I agree with you completely. This situation has gone on far too long. And you are right; I must take drastic measures because I am afraid things are getting completely out of hand." Dr. Applegate pressed the intercom button. "Mrs. Stanfield, could you come in here, please?"

Mrs. Stanfield came into the room. "Yes, Doctor?"

"Could you fix Matron Carruthers a cup of tea, please?"

"Of course." Turning to her, Mrs. Stanfield asked, "How do you take your tea?"

"Milk and two sugars."

Mrs. Stanfield left the room.

"Now, Matron, I will stay with you until the tea arrives. But then I am afraid I must leave you. My apologies. It is turning out to be a very busy afternoon for me. Mrs. Stanfield will be with you while you drink your tea. Don't feel the need to hurry. Just stay and try to relax. I want you to take a break. I will be back as soon as I can. Please do not leave until I return," Dr. Applegate said.

"I should really get back to the floor," Matron Carruthers said. "I have been away too long as it is. Goodness knows what is happening out there without me to direct my nurses."

"The patient load on your floor is very light this afternoon. The rest of your staff can manage. Right now, the most important thing is for you to sit back and relax for a few minutes. You need to get yourself to rights before you go back on the floor. Now tell me, how long have you been here at the hospital?"

"A little over twenty-two years, Dr. Applegate."

"And have you been the matron all that time?"

Matron Carruthers sat a little taller in her chair. "I worked my way up to that position. I was given the title when I came to this floor twelve years ago, just before you came on staff as chief of the junior doctors."

"Ah." Dr. Applegate smiled. "That's right. I remember that you were already here when I came. So you outrank me in terms of seniority on this floor."

A smile appeared on her face. "Yes," she said thoughtfully, "I guess I do."

There was a knock on the door. "Come in," Dr. Applegate called out. Seeing that it was Mrs. Stanfield bringing in the tea service, he scooped up the files from his desktop, stood up, and walked over to Mrs. Stanfield, who was setting the service down on the credenza that set up against the wall. He spoke to her in a low voice. "After you serve the tea, a word, please." Then walking to the door, he said, "Matron Carruthers, enjoy your tea. I shall return."

Dr. Applegate walked out of the office. He walked back to the reception area where Harold was sitting. Harold stood up and was about to say something, when Dr. Applegate put his finger up to his own lips, indicating that Harold should remain silent. Soon, Mrs. Stanfield came out and joined the little group. Dr. Applegate spoke quietly. "Mrs. Stanfield, I need you to stay with Matron Carruthers until I return. It is very important that she not leave my office. Get yourself a cup and join her for tea. Keep the conversation light and just let her talk. If she gets on the subject of Dr. Senty, then change the subject. I don't want her working herself up again."

"Yes, Doctor, I understand," Mrs. Stanfield said and immediately went into the kitchen area.

Dr. Applegate then turned to Harold and motioned for Harold to follow him out into the hallway. As they walked toward the junior doctors' lounge, Dr. Applegate said, "Please, do not say anything to Dr. Senty about what you just witnessed. No reason to get her upset."

Harold said, "Basil, I am sorry if I caused any of this trouble."

Dr. Applegate replied, "No, no, it was nothing you said or did. For now, I think it best if you stayed in the junior doctors' lounge. By all means, you would be welcome to watch the pleurocentesis, but I think we should find a doctor's coat for you so you blend in a little bit more around here."

CHAPTER 20

DR. APPLEGATE TAKES ACTION

Walking into the lounge, they found Mary Elizabeth and Dr. Connor Ramsey at the table. Drs. Batra, Westby, and Harrington were sitting on the sofa sipping tea. The young doctors all looked up when they entered the room.

Dr. Applegate said, "I would like to introduce to you my good friend and classmate from medical school, Dr. Harold Merton. He will be observing Dr. Senty's procedure. Dr. Harrington?"

"Yes, Dr. Applegate," Stuey said as he rose from the couch.

"Dr. Harrington, I am wondering if Dr. Merton might borrow one of your lab coats for the afternoon," Dr. Applegate said.

"Of course." Stuey went right to his locker and produced the white coat. Handing it to Dr. Merton, he said, "Happy to lend it to you."

"Thank you," Harold said as he put it on.

Dr. Applegate continued, "Now, were any of you planning on observing the pleurocentesis this afternoon?"

All hands went up.

"Glad to see it. Drs. Batra and Ramsey, something has come up for me, and I am unable to make it. I am wondering if you would be in charge of the younger juniors who will also be in attendance. After the procedure is over, please assemble them in the conference room. Dr. Senty, when you can, I would like you to join them to do a Q&A with the juniors. Dr. Fleming, our pulmonary specialist, will only be in attendance for the procedure. He has a full schedule this afternoon. Dr. Merton will be staying here for the rest of the afternoon. He is the GP for the village of Bellechester with over thirty years' experience.

For those of you who will be going into private practice, he would be a good resource to tap. I am sure Dr. Merton will not mind answering your questions. Now, if you will excuse me, a situation has arisen that needs my immediate attention." He turned and left the room.

When Dr. Applegate left the junior doctors' lounge, he went down to the fifth floor to see Dr. Jacob Rosen, the hospital psychiatrist. Dr. Rosen's office was set up like his was, with an outer office and a secretary. Dr. Applegate walked in the door and greeted the young, dark-haired secretary. "Good afternoon, Miss O'Malley. May I see Dr. Rosen regarding an urgent matter, please?"

The secretary smiled at him and said, "Good afternoon to you too, Dr. Applegate. It looks like Dr. Rosen is on the phone, but if you care to take a seat, I will let him know you are here. May I get you something to drink while you wait?"

"No, thank you," Dr. Applegate said as he took a seat in the waiting room. While he waited, he opened the file and read again some of his notes and some of the memos that Nurse Matron Carruthers had left for him regarding Dr. Senty.

It was only a few minutes of waiting, but to Dr. Applegate, the wait seemed much longer. He could hear Miss O'Malley on the phone saying, "Dr. Rosen, Dr. Applegate is here regarding an urgent matter. Yes, Doctor."

Hanging up the phone, she said to him, "Dr. Applegate, if you will please follow me. Dr. Rosen can see you now."

Dr. Applegate got up and said, "Thank you, Miss O'Malley."

Miss O'Malley led Dr. Applegate into the inner office. Dr. Rosen stood up from behind his desk. Dr. Rosen was a short man with a head of curly brown hair and a full beard. He wore a pair of round spectacles with brown frames on a chain around his neck. Pointing to the chair in front of his desk, he said, "Here, sit down, Basil. What brings you to see me on such a pressing errand?" Turning to Miss O'Malley, he said, "Thank you, that will be all."

"Very good, Doctor." Miss O'Malley shut the door behind her.

Dr. Applegate sat down in the chair with the thick file in his lap. "Jacob, I am at my wit's end with Matron Carruthers."

"Let me guess," Dr. Rosen said. "She is complaining about Dr. Senty again."

"Yes, this week alone, she has written me three pages on Dr. Senty's improper treatment of one of our patients, and this afternoon, she burst into my office with more complaints about Dr. Senty. In my estimation, the situation has escalated to the point where I fear for the woman's mental health."

"Doesn't Dr. Senty leave on Friday?"

"Yes, she does. But I am worried that the matron's attitude toward Dr. Senty is not just a clash of personalities. I think there is more to it, but I would only be speculating, which is why I have come to ask you to lend your expertise in this matter."

"Thank you, Basil, for your vote of confidence. I'm glad to help out in any way I can."

"On Friday, as you know, we have the Welcome Luncheon for the new cohort that will be starting their junior training here at Mercy. I am concerned that we get to the bottom of Matron Carruthers's treatment of Dr. Senty because there is another female in this new cohort. And I don't think I could go through this again for another four years."

"Yes, I see. What would you like me to do?" Dr. Rosen asked.

Dr. Applegate said, "I would like you to read through this file. It contains all her notes to me and my notes on her complaints of Dr. Senty from the past year. I would also like you to talk to her to get your assessment of the whole situation. Finally, I would like you to offer your prescription of what we need to do to move forward."

"Of course, I can do that. Where is she now?" Dr. Rosen asked.

"Hopefully, she is still in my office drinking tea. I have Mrs. Stanfield with her, keeping an eye on her. In her present state, I cannot in good conscience have her return to duty on the floor."

"Here's what I will do. I will come back to your office with you and see if she will come down to my office. We will talk and go from there. How does that sound?"

"Thank you, Jacob. That sounds like a good plan." Dr. Applegate rose from his chair and handed the file over to Dr. Rosen.

When the doctors returned to Dr. Applegate's office, Matron Carruthers and Mrs. Stanfield had finished their tea and were talking about the high price of hosiery.

Dr. Rosen went to Matron Carruthers and took her hand. "Good afternoon, Matron Carruthers. Very nice to see you again."

"And you too, Dr. Rosen," the nurse said in a surprised voice.

He then went over to where Mrs. Stanfield was sitting. "Mrs. Stanfield, always a pleasure."

"Dr. Rosen." Mrs. Stanfield got up and removed the tea service and herself from the room.

When the trio was alone, Dr. Applegate said, "I know you have had many concerns about Dr. Senty this week. I am sorry that you were unaware that Mr. Merton is actually my dear friend and classmate, Dr. Harold Merton. He came to Mercy on a quest to find a young doctor to join him in his practice in the village of Bellechester. I admitted him as a patient so that he could better assess the junior doctors' abilities and their bedside manner."

"Well, Dr. Applegate, I should have known this information sooner," Matron Carruthers said.

"I am afraid I could not reveal that information, because when Dr. Merton was admitted as a patient, I was bound by the doctor-patient privilege. Nevertheless, I have become increasingly concerned over your constant criticism of Dr. Senty. While several matrons have lodged their concerns over my junior doctors during this past year, it appears that you have singled out Dr. Senty and directed all your criticism toward her. I will admit that Dr. Senty has made a few errors in judgment in her dealings with patients. However, the majority of your criticism did not warrant any intervention from me. I feel you are judging her most unjustly, which is why I would like you to talk with Dr. Rosen."

"Begging your pardon, Doctor, but why would I do that?" she asked. "I was not aware that Dr. Rosen has any supervisory authority over Dr. Senty."

Dr. Applegate said, "You are correct. I, and I alone, bear responsibility for Dr. Senty, as well as the other junior doctors. However, in this matter, I am afraid that I am no longer impartial. I have asked Dr. Rosen to offer us a fresh perspective. He will listen to your concerns and then offer suggestions as to how we can best move forward. How does that sound to you?"

"Well, if you think it will do any good. But what about my shift? I am supposed to be on duty. I cannot afford to take time off."

"Don't worry about your shift. There is more than adequate staff to cover the patients we have at present. Right now, your duty is to talk with Dr. Rosen. I will see to it that you will be credited for a full shift tonight," Dr. Applegate said.

"That is very good of you, Dr. Applegate."

Dr. Rosen stood next to her and offered her his hand. "Shall we?"

Matron Carruthers took his hand and silently got up from her chair.

Dr. Applegate said, "Thank you, Matron," as he escorted Dr. Rosen and Matron Carruthers from his office.

So as not to draw undue attention to themselves, Matron Carruthers and Dr. Rosen walked to the end of the hallway and took the stairs down two flights to the fifth floor, bypassing the nurses' station and the lifts.

After they left his office, Dr. Applegate went to the kitchenette, where Mrs. Stanfield was cleaning up after serving tea. She had worked for Dr. Applegate for all twelve years he had been at this hospital. He didn't even have to ask. He knew he could count on her discretion regarding the events of this afternoon.

Dr. Applegate said, "So sorry I had to involve you in this situation."

"That is quite all right, Doctor. I hope Dr. Rosen will be able to help," Mrs. Stanfield said.

Dr. Applegate said, "In light of today's events, how would it be if you took Friday afternoon off? With pay, of course. I will be at the Welcome Luncheon, and so will all the fourth-years for most of the afternoon."

Mrs. Stanfield said, "Why, thank you, Doctor. That would be a treat."

CHAPTER 21

$\mathcal{D}$R. SENTY IN THE SPOTLIGHT

In the junior doctors' lounge, Mary Elizabeth looked at her watch. She got up from the table and said, "Looks like I will see everyone in Mr. Baxter's room." She walked to the nurses' station.

Nurse Daly greeted her. "Dr. Senty, Mr. Baxter has received his extra pain medication, and we have your instrument tray here if you would care to look it over."

"Yes, thank you. Isn't Matron Carruthers on this afternoon? I thought I saw her earlier," Mary Elizabeth said.

"Dr. Applegate just came by and said that Matron was not feeling well and that I should take her place for the rest of her shift."

"I hope she will be feeling better soon. And I am sure you will do a fine job tonight as head nurse." Mary Elizabeth went back to looking at the tray and doing the procedure in her mind. She said, "It looks like everything is here. Thank you."

"Do you want a nurse with you?" Nurse Daly asked.

"Yes, and I am also going to need the assistance of an orderly. Could you please call one for me?"

"Yes, Doctor."

"It is going to be quite crowded in that room as it is. There will be more doctors in that room than at the golf course on a summer's day," Mary Elizabeth said under her breath.

Picking up the tray, Mary Elizabeth started down the hall. Knocking on the door of room 723, she walked in. "Good afternoon, Mr. Baxter. Are you ready to be the star of the show?"

"I don't know about that, but I am ready to be able to breathe without pain," Mr. Baxter said.

"The most difficult part of this procedure today is going to be getting you into the correct position. Your broken leg is presenting us with a challenge, but I think we can overcome it by rearranging some furniture in your room."

There was a knock on the door, and an orderly and nurse walked into the room. Mary Elizabeth gave them instructions, and in no time, they had Mr. Baxter seated on the edge of his bed. His broken leg extended onto a chair filled with pillows. Adjusting the tray table with more pillows for cushions, Mr. Baxter was able to lean forward. Mary Elizabeth untied his hospital gown and marked a spot on his back where she would insert the needle.

By now, the junior doctors, her cohort, Dr. Merton, and Dr. Fleming, the senior pulmonologist, were now gathered around. Mary Elizabeth began by introducing Mr. Baxter and giving a brief synopsis of his condition. Then methodically, she explained what she was going to do. The procedure went smoothly, the fluid was drained, and in thirty minutes, it was all over.

Mary Elizabeth asked Dr. Fleming whether he would like to make any comments.

He said, "Dr. Senty, your pleurocentesis was textbook. Very well done, considering you had to deal with Mr. Baxter's broken leg. Doctors, I hope you took note of how she positioned her patient. Very important. Now, a sample of the fluid will be sent to the lab for further testing, just to rule out any additional disease. Considering that Mr. Baxter was in a motorcycle accident, it is most likely that his fluid buildup was caused by a traumatic blow to his chest. I am sorry that I cannot join your debriefing, but I am sure that Dr. Senty will be able to answer your questions. Good afternoon." He then left the room. Drs. Batra and Ramsey took the junior doctors back to the conference room. Dr. Merton followed.

The orderly, nurse, and Mary Elizabeth got Mr. Baxter settled back in bed and the furniture set to right again.

"Thank you, Mr. Jones, for your help. Please take this sample down to the lab," Mary Elizabeth said.

"Yes, Doctor."

"Nurse, after I leave, please take his vitals every hour until 10:00 p.m. I want to be sure he stays stable."

After the nurse and orderly left the room, Dr. Senty listened to Mr. Baxter's heart and lungs. "Mr. Baxter, how do you feel? Your heart and lungs sound good. The procedure was not too uncomfortable for you, was it?"

"Not too bad. The most painful part was when you jabbed me with that numbing medicine. That did sting. But after that, I did not feel a thing. You were right, Dr. Senty, I do feel much better. No more pain when I breathe." He paused for a moment and then said, "You know, you are a very good teacher. Even I learned something today."

Mary Elizabeth laughed. "Thank you for the compliment, but I will leave the teaching to my two sisters and one of my brothers. They are the teachers in my family. Now, as you heard, the nurse will be checking in on you for a while, but then you should have an undisturbed night. I want to make sure you get a good night's sleep tonight. I will see you tomorrow morning at rounds when I will introduce you to your new doctor. You have a good evening."

As she turned to go, Mr. Baxter became alarmed. He called out, "Wait! What?! New doctor? Aren't you going to be my doctor anymore?"

Mary Elizabeth went back and sat down in the chair next to his bed. "Mr. Baxter, my time at Mother of Mercy Hospital is over on Friday. For my cohort, it is the changing of the guard. All of us will have finished our program, and a new set of doctors will be taking over our patients tomorrow. Now, I have to go. But I promise that before I leave tomorrow, we will have time to say a proper goodbye. How does that sound?"

"You won't forget?" Mr. Baxter asked.

"No, I won't forget. If you like, you can remind me tomorrow morning when I come in with your new doctor."

"Okay, I will. Say, do you know who my new doctor will be?"

"No, I don't. Dr. Applegate will make the announcement tomorrow morning. Rounds won't begin until after nine, so you can sleep in a little later tomorrow. See you then."

Mary Elizabeth hurried to the conference room where Ruhan and Connor were fielding questions from the junior doctors. Mary Elizabeth put Mr. Baxter's X-rays on the light box and then answered more questions. After the last junior doctor left, it was just Drs. Batra, Ramsey, and Merton left in the room.

"Thanks, guys, for taking care of the juniors," Mary Elizabeth said.

"Nice job, Mary Elizabeth," Ruhan said.

"You looked like you do that procedure every day. Well done," Connor said.

"Do you want to walk with us to the India Palace? We will be leaving as soon as we are done here," Ruhan said.

"Thanks, but you guys go on ahead. I just have one more meeting, and then I will join you. Save me a place and order me one of those mango lassis that I like."

Connor laughed. "One mango lassi for the lassie, coming right up."

CHAPTER 22

*T*HE PROPOSAL

Mary Elizabeth and Harold were now alone in the conference room. "Would you like some tea?" Mary Elizabeth asked.

Harold said, "Only if you are having a cup."

"Yes, I would like some. If next door is empty, we could talk there. Otherwise, we could come back here."

All the junior doctors had already left for the day, so the lounge was empty. After they filled their cups, Mary Elizabeth said, "Do you mind if we sit at the table? I'm afraid if I sat on the sofa, I would fall asleep."

"The table is fine."

As they sat down, Harold said, "Emme, there is something we have not talked about, and Basil says it doesn't matter, but I think it does. I know this is personal, but I have to ask you something. May I?"

"Of course, Harold. You can ask me anything." Mary Elizabeth looked across the table and saw how he moved forward in his chair. He had both hands around his cup, and the lines in his face deepened.

Dr. Applegate walked into the lounge just in time to hear Harold say, "Emme, do you want to get married?"

Harold's question stopped Dr. Applegate in his tracks. He looked at Mary Elizabeth, who was facing the door. Mary Elizabeth's eyes grew wide. Putting her cup down, she looked first to Dr. Applegate and then into Harold's brown eyes and asked, "Harold, are you asking me to marry you?"

Before he could reply, Dr. Applegate said, "I should leave you two alone for a few minutes.

Harold, I will be in my office." With that, he beat a hasty retreat right out the door again.

Seeing the reaction to his question, first from Basil and then from Mary Elizabeth, Harold looked confused. "Me? Marry you? Oh no, Emme. Oh my." Replaying his question in his head, it suddenly dawned on him how his question was received by both Mary Elizabeth and Basil. He got flustered. "Oh, Emme. It's not that I wouldn't like to marry you. Maybe if I were thirty years younger and if I knew you better. Oh my! But no. I wasn't asking you in particular. Oh my, I really put my foot into it this time. Emme, I am sorry if you thought . . ."

Seeing Harold in such genuine distress, Mary Elizabeth dared not laugh. She reached across the table and patted Harold's hand. "It's okay. I see now that you were just asking me in general if I have ever thought about marriage. Is that right?"

Harold decided it would be best if he just stopped talking. He nodded.

"It is a fair question, Harold. I guess I always thought my goal of becoming a doctor and being married and having children were mutually exclusive. I could never quite figure out how to make it all work. I thought I had to make a choice. And I did. I decided to concentrate on my studies and not get serious with any young man. In college and in medical school, I had seen too many women give up on their careers to become wives and mothers. They seem happy enough. But I knew that life was not for me. I could never live with myself if I didn't try to see how far I could go in my dream to become a doctor."

Harold said, "What about now that you have come to the end of your training? Does the picture look any different for you?"

"Really, my training is just going to end on Friday. No, getting married is still the furthest thing from my mind," Mary Elizabeth said. "Now, Harold, don't take this the wrong way, but," she said with a smile, "after being around doctors for so long, the last person I want to marry is a doctor."

"I guess I am relieved to hear it. I just didn't want you to get your hopes up. I am afraid that there are not a lot of eligible bachelors in Bellechester."

"What?" Mary Elizabeth cried. "No handsome dukes? No rich, widowed, landed gentry with a fevered brow that I could nurse back to health, and in gratitude, he would whisk me away to his estate, where we would spend the rest of our lives in the lap of luxury?"

"I'm afraid you have been reading too many Barbara Cartland novels, Emme."

"Actually, it was Jane Austen. In college, Sister Paul Marie taught a class on her novels. It was one of my favorite classes."

"Sorry to disappoint you," Harold said.

"That's fine. I'm not looking for a husband right now. I just want to concentrate on being the best doctor I can be and put all my education and training to use," Mary Elizabeth said. "My philosophy on matters of the heart is just like that song that Doris Day sings on the radio, you know, 'Qué Será, Será.'"

Harold smiled, "Ah yes."

"No cause for concern. I am quite content as I am."

"Do you have any more questions about the job?" Harold asked.

"Just one more, Harold. How do you feel about practicing preventable medicine?" Mary Elizabeth asked.

"You mean like vaccines?" Harold asked.

"Yes, but also to try to do a little public education too so that people don't get sick in the first place."

Harold said, "That sounds nice, but honestly, besides vaccines, I have not had the time for that. It is all I can do these days to keep up with my patient load. But if you would like to try to do some public health education, I will not stand in your way."

"Of course, treating our sick patients comes first, but I just thought that maybe I could work with the schools and the women's group and try to keep people healthy as well as treat the sick."

"Emme, did you just say 'our patients'? Does that mean that you will come to Bellechester?" Harold asked.

"Before I give you my final answer, I just have to be sure. So I will ask you one more time, are you sure you want me? I can be headstrong and stubborn. What if the people of Bellechester will not accept me? I don't want you to ever feel that you are stuck with me."

"Emme, if it would make you feel better, Basil had an idea. He proposed that we have a trial period."

"Trial period? What kind of trial period?" Mary Elizabeth asked.

"Well, how long would it take for you to know if Bellechester is a good fit for you? One month? Six?"

"Three months sounds reasonable," Mary Elizabeth said. "Maybe you will decide you don't like working with me. What do you think?"

"Three months sounds good to me too. Do we have an agreement?" Harold asked.

Mary Elizabeth stood up. She turned to Harold and stuck out her hand. "Dr. Merton, we have a deal. I will be happy to join your practice in Bellechester."

Harold also stood up, and they shook hands. "Very pleased to have you, Dr. Senty."

Mary Elizabeth said, "I will plan to be in Bellechester by Sunday evening. If anything changes, I will let you know."

"Very good. Now," Harold said as he removed his white lab coat, "can you see that this coat gets returned to Dr. Harrington?"

"Of course. I will just put it back in his locker," Mary Elizabeth said as she took the coat and opened his locker.

"I'd better be going." Harold smiled. "I believe I owe Basil an explanation."

"Yes, please." Mary Elizabeth laughed. "Dr. Applegate could not have walked in at a worse time. If you don't show up pretty soon, I am afraid he will think we are busy planning our wedding." Mary Elizabeth opened her locker and hung up her coat and took out her purse.

"At least, I will have an interesting story to tell at dinner tonight," Harold said. "Are you ready to go join your colleagues?"

"I have to write in Mr. Baxter's chart, and then I will join them. Tonight we are celebrating Dr. Connor Ramsey's job appointment. He will be working for the Medical Research Council," Mary Elizabeth said.

"That is a very prestigious post. Will you be telling them about your new job?"

"Not tonight," Mary Elizabeth said. "There will be time for that tomorrow. I don't want to take anything away from Connor. He has always been the quietest one of our group. No, tonight is his night to shine." As Mary Elizabeth walked to the door, she stopped and turned around. "You know, Harold, I will miss saying the Rosary with you tonight. Do you know why?"

Harold got a smile on his face. "I think I do. Tonight is the Glorious Mysteries, isn't it?"

"Yes. Today has been a glorious day. Good evening, Harold," Mary Elizabeth said.

CHAPTER 23

AN EVENING WITH FRIENDS

Leaving the junior doctor's lounge, Harold walked down to Dr. Applegate's office. The outer door to his office was open, as Mrs. Stanfield had already left for the day. Basil was at his desk.

When he saw Harold, he said, "Have you finished all your business with Dr. Senty? Are congratulations in order for the two of you?"

"Yes, Basil, I have. And yes, congratulations are in order," Harold said with a wide grin. "I will tell all at supper tonight. Now, let's go see that beautiful bride of yours," he said as he picked up his suitcase.

Even though the woman who greeted them at the door had white hair and a wrinkled face, in Harold's eyes, Caroline was still the young, vivacious, blond-haired coed who was always so much fun to be around. Even after Basil and Caroline started to go together, they often included Harold in their plans.

Tonight, Caroline had made a delicious roast beef supper with all the trimmings. Harold made a toast to their friendship of over forty years. Basil toasted that Harold's trip to London had been a rousing success. During the meal, Harold told Caroline the story of Basil overhearing him proposing to Dr. Senty. They all had a good laugh over that one. The evening passed quickly as it does when old friends get together.

The next morning after breakfast, Caroline Applegate drove Harold to the train station. Harold said, "Thank you for a wonderful meal last night and for putting me up for the night. I truly enjoyed your hospitality."

"Next time, please don't stay away so long. Come and see us again. Basil and I loved having you."

"Being with you and talking about old times, well, I feel thirty years younger this morning."

"You know, your visit has been good for Basil too. The pressures of his job have been weighing on him particularly hard lately. Last night was the first time in a long time that he truly looked relaxed. I thank you for that."

"Well, if you ever need to get away for a while, come see me in Bellechester. The Shropshire Hills are beautiful. I would love to show them to you. My place is large enough for you to stay. I would like to return the hospitality."

"Thank you. I would indeed love to see the place that has kept you these past thirty plus years. Seeing that you took some time off, maybe Basil will be more amenable to taking some time off too. Oh, here we are already." Caroline stopped the car in front of Paddington Station. Harold got out and retrieved his suitcase from the back seat.

He disappeared into the station. In twenty minutes, the train pulled out from the station with one very happy man on board. His mission to find a young doctor to join him in Bellechester had been accomplished. But what made him smile was that he could not wait to tell his best friend, Father Evenson, about all his adventures in London. It had truly been a memorable trip. He settled back in his seat next to the window and enjoyed the view. No more worries. He was going home to his beloved Bellechester.

AFTERWORD

If you enjoyed reading this book, be sure to look for the next one in the series, *Trouble Comes to Bellechester*. In the sequel, we find out what happens when Dr. Mary Elizabeth Senty joins Dr. Harold Merton's medical practice in the small rural village in the Shropshire Hills. There will be many new characters to meet, including Father Mathias Evenson and the newly appointed head of Bellechester's police department, Chief Inspector William Francis Donnelly. Mary Elizabeth has clearly stated she does not have romance or marriage on her mind. But what about

Chief Inspector Donnelly? What is on his mind? All will be revealed in *Trouble Comes to Bellechester*.

$\mathcal{D}$ISCUSSION QUESTIONS

1. Who is your favorite character and why?

2. As both Basil and Mary Elizabeth point out, there were easier ways for Harold to find a doctor to join him in his medical practice. What do you think about the way he chose? What does that say about him?

3. In their first meeting, neither Mary Elizabeth nor Harold revealed their true identities. Do you think this had any effect on their friendship? Why or why not? As their friendship developed, why did they

find it so difficult to tell each other the truth?

4. Mary Elizabeth felt frustration at not being given the chance to prove what she could do because of her gender. Have you ever had a similar experience of not being given a chance because your gender, race, age, or education? How did it make you feel? How did you deal with the situation?

5. What are your thoughts and feelings toward Matron Carruthers? Basil believes that there is some deep underlying cause in Matron's criticism of Mary Elizabeth. Do you agree or disagree? What do you think of the way Basil handled the situation? How would you have handled it?

6. At the end of the story, what options does Mary Elizabeth face in deciding her future?

7. If you were Mary Elizabeth, what would you decide? Why?

8. The story takes place in 1959. Is Mary Elizabeth justified in her concern of what

the villagers would think if she shared the Doctor's residence with Harold? Do you think the opinion of the villagers would matter to her as much if the story took place in the present day? Why or why not?

9. In this story, our heroine is known by many names: Dr. Senty, Mary Elizabeth, Emme, Maria Elisabetta. Take a few minutes to think about and list all the names that have identified you in your life. Which ones have meant the most to you and why? By what name does God call you?

10. For both Mary Elizabeth and Harold prayer is an important part of their daily life. What are some of your spiritual practices that connect you with the Divine?

11. What impact does Mary Elizabeth make in Harold's life? What does Harold mean to Mary Elizabeth? Name a person who has made a difference in your life.

$\mathcal{A}$CKNOWLEDGMENTS

Do dreams come true? For me, writing this book is a dream come true. I have been writing stories since the age of ten. But these were private stories as a way to amuse myself. In high school, I did muster the courage to take a creative writing class. Mrs. Stifter, of happy memory was my first writing coach. I got the courage to submit one article for the school paper. What a thrill it was to see it in print. That was the one and only article, for in high school and for most of my life, I have wrestled with those twin killers of dreams, fear and doubt.

It was at that same high school, Archbishop Brady, where I discovered that those required religion classes ignited a passion within me to pursue the study of theology at the undergraduate and graduate levels. That led to a twenty five year career working in parishes and for the Archdiocese of Minneapolis and St. Paul. But like those persistent dandelions that pop up in my lawn, in my gardens and between the cracks of the sidewalk, the dream of becoming an author never went away.

Many years later, a small notice in the local newspaper advertised a workshop at my local library. I believe the title was – *So You Want to Be a Writer*. Feeling abnormally courageous, I attended the workshop. The presenter, James Silas Rogers, an English professor at a local university shared his expertise and encouraged the class to begin writing. If someone who grew up in my hometown, and the brother of my high school classmate can become a successful published author, maybe there was hope for me too. I am very grateful to Jim and to the librarians at the South St. Paul Public Library for offering that workshop. Thank you. And to all aspiring writers out there, take advantage of the programs at your local library and support their work. They are invaluable institutions in our communities.

Do you recall the story of Cinderella? She had a dream of going to the ball and meeting the handsome prince. But to make that dream become a reality, she needed the assistance of a fairy godmother. With a little magic, six white mice became a team of horses, a pumpkin turned into a carriage, and rats grew into a footman and a groomsman. Everything and everyone worked together to make Cinderella's dream come true.

It turns out it would take several fairy godmothers, armed with the magic of expertise, to make my dream of writing and publishing a book come true. I would like to thank the following generous, amazing people for their help. I am grateful to my beta readers, Amber, Luschka, Abagail, and Belle Grace, for sharing their comments. Their critiques helped me craft a better story. Knowing I wanted work with a local publisher, I talked to Becca Hart at Beaver's Pond Press. Her friendly and encouraging voice walked me through the initial application process and arranged for a meeting with the leader of the Pond, Lily Coyle. I am still not quite sure why Lily took a chance on this novice writer, but she did. I dove into the Pond and have never regretted it. She has a wonderful group of talented women working with her, and to all of them I owe a debt of gratitude. I knew I was in good hands when Lily introduced me to my project manager, Tina Brackins, another Archbishop Brady alum. Go Broncos!!! Tina has been a steady, gentle guide through the many steps of turning this manuscript into a book. Courtney King Bain did a fantastic editing job. She had no small task as she corrected all my grammatical errors. They were legion! ScriptAcuity Studio did the final proof and gave the text that extra polish. The cover illustration was done by Lisa Kosmo. Her beautiful artwork captured the setting and the spirit of the main characters. Was it her cover that first enticed you to pick up this book?

I would like to thank my family for their unending support and understanding during my crazy, self-imposed writing schedule, and my friends for their prayers and words of encouragement.

And finally, I would like to thank you, the reader for taking a chance on this first-time author. I hope I do not disappoint in providing you with an enjoyable story. Do dreams come true? Yes! The proof is in your hands. Now what dreams do you have? I pray you will find the godmothers and godfathers you need to help you make your dreams come true.

$\mathcal{A}$BOUT THE AUTHOR

Margaret A. Blenkush lives in Minnesota and enjoys retirement, gardening, volunteering, sudoku puzzles and the changing seasons. She shares her home with her nephew and two pet rabbits, Nick and Nora. A lifelong Catholic, she is also an Oblate of St. Benedict's Monastery, St. Joseph, Minnesota. Although she has been writing stories since she was ten, The *Doctor of Bellechester* is her first book.

Sunday, August 30, 1959, Bellechester, UK

PREVIEW:

*T*ROUBLE COMES TO BELLECHESTER
Book 2 of the M. E. Senty Series

Father Matthias Evenson walked up the few short streets from the rectory to the large building on Abbey Road which served as the home and office of Bellechester's General Practitioner, Dr. Harold Merton. Father Evenson had a standing appointment every Sunday evening with him not for any medical reason but for their weekly supper and cribbage game.

"How about a sherry before we begin the next game?" Harold asked. It's not often that I beat you like that. I think that calls for a celebration." Harold went over to the buffet and poured out two glasses from the crystal decanter. He handed one to Matt and picking his glass up he proposed the following toast; "To adventures taken and new ones to come. Cheers!"

"Cheers!" Matt took a sip. "Harold, I must say that you are like a changed man since you have returned from London on Thursday. I have never seen you so happy."

"Matt, I never knew what a change of scenery could do for a fellow."

Matt said, "We toasted to adventures. Are you going to tell me about your trip? You haven't said much about it since you have returned and you were very mysterious about where you were going before you left."

Harold teased, "I thought you liked mysteries. Besides, I promised ..." and then he fell silent and took another sip of sherry.

Matt perked up like a hound that just caught a scent. "Promised. What promise? Who did you promise?" He was so excited; he almost fell off his chair.

"I do believe it is whom," Harold corrected. He just smiled.

Matt sat back in his chair. "You are enjoying toying with me, aren't you?"

"Yes, I am, very much." Then he inquired in a serious tone, "Do you have your stole with you?"

"Of course. It's in my pocket. I always carry it in case of emergencies."

"Well, put it on."

"What! You want to go to confession, here and now? In the middle of our card game? I just heard your confession yesterday."

"I know. I do want to tell you about my trip, but I need to know that you are not going to say anything to anyone, especially to your house-keeper, Martha. If she gets wind of it, the news will be all over Bellechester by morning. No, you must keep my secret. And if I tell you under the seal of the confessional, well, then I can be abso-lutely assured of your secrecy."

"I am perfectly capable of holding a confidence without dragging Holy Mother Church into it," Matt said with a hint of indignation.

"For now, all I will tell you is that I went to London to find a young doctor to assist me in my practice. If last winter taught me anything, it taught me that I should have some back up just in case, you know..."

"Yes, we were all so worried about whether you would pull through from your bout with pneumonia last February. So, did you find someone?'"

A peculiar smile came upon Harold's face. "Oh yes, I did find someone, …

"You don't say. Tell me about the new doctor who is coming to Bellechester."

"Well, the doctor is young; I'd say early thirties, very qualified, passed all the examinations, received glowing recommendations from instructors and has a very compassionate bedside manner."

"Yes, that is all very good, but what is the new doctor like, his personality. Is he married?"

"No, the doctor is not married. Yes, I think you two will get along just fine; you both like to laugh a lot."

"Getting information out of you is more difficult than pulling teeth." Matt was growing exasperated. "Anything else?"

"Oh, you will like this. The doctor is a practicing Catholic. So, I am sure you will have ample opportunity to do a proper Inquisition later." Harold said with a smile.

"Very amusing," Matt said.

"That is all I am going to say for now. You will have to wait until I introduce you. According to the telegram I received yesterday, Bellechester's new doctor will be arriving tomorrow. Now, let's get back to playing cribbage. I do believe it is your deal. More sherry?" He held up the decanter.